The Terridae?

Dumarest felt the cold shock of belated recognition. The ending implied resemblance. An affinity with what went before. Terr. Terra? And Terra was another name for Earth!

"Two minutes," said Volodya.

Dumarest ignored him as he considered the implications. The caskets decorated with their symbols: the signs of the zodiac which signposted Earth. Caskets used by the Terridae? Guarded by others of the same conviction?

Would Volodya willingly destroy his own?

"One minute," he said and Dumarest heard the sharp intake of breath. "Fifty-five seconds." An eternity and then, "I must insist on your answer."

One which had to be correct or Dumarest would die, tasting the bitter irony of losing what he had searched for so long to find only in the final moment.

He said, "I do not beg for life—I demand you give it. Demand, too, your hospitality and protection—things it is your duty to provide . . ."

". . . For I am of Earth."

The
TERRIDAE

E. C. Tubb

DAW BOOKS, INC.
Donald A. Wollheim, Publisher

1633 Broadway, New York, N.Y. 10019

DEDICATION

To Frank Arnold

FIRST PRINTING, OCTOBER 1981

1 2 3 4 5 6 7 8 9

 DAW TRADEMARK REGISTERED
U.S. PAT. OFF. MARCA
REGISTRADA. HECHO EN U.S.A.

PRINTED IN U.S.A.

Chapter One

——◆——◆——◆——

He was small, brown, dressed in a jupon of scarlet edged with silver, a pointed cap on a rich tangle of curls and striped hose on slender legs, a boy of about ten now caught in a mesh of brambles with one foot snared in the clamped jaws of a vegetable trap. On each wrist captive bells made a harsh jangling as he waved his arms.

Dumarest had heard the sound as he crested the ridge and tracked it to its source lower down the slope. Now, halting, he eased the weight of the pack on his shoulders.

"Are you hurt?" Dumarest frowned as the boy shook his head. "Can't you speak?"

Again the shake of the head, this time accompanied by the thrust of a finger toward the opened mouth. A mute, trapped in a prison of thorns, the bells his only means of calling for help. Yet would such a boy be out alone?

Dumarest turned, eyes narrowed as he scanned the area. On all sides the ground fell from the encircling hills to cup the solitary town of Shard in a spined embrace. Matted grass broken with tall fronds bright with lacelike blooms inter-mingled with rearing brambles. Sprawling growths reared twice the height of a man, bearing succulent berries and traps designed to snare insects and small rodents. The branches and stems, some as thick as a man's body, were covered with curved and vicious barbs.

"Don't move!" Dumarest called the warning as, again, the air shook to the desperate jangle of bells. "Just stay calm. I'll get you out."

5

He studied the ground as the lad obeyed, noting marks in the matted grass, the lie of stems. To one side a thorned branch had been broken and sap oozed from the fracture. As he knelt to check for tracks he heard a soft rustle and spun, snatching at the knife he carried in his boot, sunlight splintering from the nine inches of edged and pointed steel.

A rustle, followed by others as a gust of wind stirred the fronds and filled the somnolent air with the heady scent of their perfume.

Rising, Dumarest slipped the pack from his shoulders and eased his way toward the trapped boy. Small and lithe, the lad would have had little trouble slipping through the brambles, but three times Dumarest had to slash clear a path. As he reached the recumbent figure certain things became clear.

The jupon was of cheap material, patched, frayed, the silver edging nothing but scraps of discarded foil. The bells were of brass suspended from wires on either wrist. The hose were covered with darns and the pointed hat had been roughly made—unmistakable signs of poverty despite their bright show, matched by the hollow cheeks and the too-bright eyes, the frail bones of the boy himself. A basket to one side explained his presence, the container half-full of purple berries; a harvest painfully won.

"Steady!" The thin ankle trapped in the jaws was mottled with bruises, blood dappling the hose, evidence of frantic efforts to pull it free. The knife flashed as Dumarest cut at the tangle of thorns. "Don't move!"

Though mute, the lad could hear and understand and he remained still as Dumarest finished the task and sheathed his knife. Bells jangled as he lifted the boy and he saw the extended hand, the determination stamped on the small face.

"You want the fruit, is that it?" He recovered the basket as the lad nodded. "Here. Can you walk?" He watched as the boy took a cautious, limping step. "Too slow. I'll carry you."

A heave and the lad was riding on his shoulder, the basket held firmly in the small hands. Cautiously Dumarest retraced his path, halting as, again, he heard a soft rustle.

This time there was no wind.

A patch of grass lay to one side and Dumarest moved toward it, throwing the boy into its softness as again something rustled close. He turned, ducking. A club aimed at his head missed to whine through the air, the man holding it thrown off-balance by the unexpected lack of resistance. He was a grimy, rat-faced man wearing garments stained green and brown, camouflage protecting him from the human predators who lurked in the brush. He doubled, retching, as Dumarest kicked him in the stomach, staggering back to become hooked in thorned spines.

"Jarl?" The voice came from ahead, impatient, querulous. "You get him? You get him, Jarl?"

Two of them and there could be more. Dumarest lifted the knife from his boot and slipped to one side among the brambles feeling the rasp of thorns over his clothing, the drag and burn as a barb tore at his scalp.

"Jarl? Answer me, damn you!"

A rustle and Dumarest saw a mottled bulk, the loom of gross body, the gleam of sunlight reflected from furtive eyes. A man lunged forward, gripping a gnarled branch. His fingers parted beneath the slash of razor-edged steel to fall in spurting showers of blood.

"You bastard!" Pain and rage convulsed the ravaged face. "I'll have your eyes for that! Leave you to wander blind in the brush! Jarl! Kelly! Get him, damn you!"

He backed, his uninjured hand diving into a pocket, lifting again weighted with the bulk of a gun. A wide-barreled shot-projector which could fill the air with a lethal hail. As it appeared Dumarest threw himself forward, blade extended, the point ripping into the body below the breastbone in an upwards thrust which reached the heart. Killing as surely as the burn of a laser through the brain.

As the man fell he heard a frantic cursing, the clumsy passage of a body close at hand, the echoes of another from where he had left his pack. When he reached the spot he found it gone.

The jangle of bells reminded him of the boy.

He sat where he'd been thrown, his eyes anxious, the injured leg held stiffly before him. The ankle was too swollen for the lad to do more than crawl. Jarl had vanished, scraps of skin and clothing left hanging on broken thorns, a trail of blood marking his passage, a trail Dumarest could easily follow but not while carrying the boy. And, with darkness, other predators would come eager for helpless prey.

"Up!" Dumarest lifted the small body to his shoulder. "I'd better get you home."

The town matched the planet—small, bleak, devoid of all but functional utility. The field was an expanse of rutted dirt, deserted now, the warehouses sagging and empty. Once there had been a bustling tide of commerce but the veins of valuable ores had been exhausted, the operation closed down, sheds and workers abandoned. Among them had been the local factor.

"Earl!" He rose as Dumarest entered his store. "Man, it's good to see you!"

Mel Glover was a one-time face-worker who had been hurt in an accident and now dragged a useless foot. A big, broad man with a rugged build and a face marred with a perpetual scowl, he ran the store and acted as agent and hated every moment of it. He found surcease in talk and drugs and exotic dreams. Now he frowned as Dumarest set down the boy.

"Anton! What the devil have you been up to?" He looked at Dumarest. "He find you or what?" The frown deepened as he listened to an answer. "Caught in the brambles—anything else?"

An attempt on his life, theft, a man lying dead—but Dumarest chose not to elaborate. He said, "That's it. I heard him and found him and brought him in. You know where he lives?"

"In the Drell."

"With his people?"

"His mother. His father got himself killed last year." Glover reached into a jar and threw the boy a ball of wrapped candy. "Here, lad. Can you walk? Try hopping. Good. Off you go now." As the boy hopped away, sucking his sweet, the basket hung over one arm, he added, "I bet you didn't know he could do that."

"No."

"But you know he's a mute?"

Dumarest nodded and looked around the store. It was as he remembered, cluttered with a variety of produce, most of local manufacture. Baskets of woven reed filled with delicate blooms rested beside pots of sunbaked clay crammed with spices, seeds, sections of narcotic weed. A bale held furs, another the tanned hides of ferocious lizards, the scales seeming to be made of nacre traced with silver, jet and gold. Products of minor value but still worth collecting by ships content with small profits. Beneath a window facing the foothills stood a bench, a book lying on its surface together with a pair of powerful binoculars.

"You've been out almost a month," said Glover. "I was beginning to get anxious. Any luck?"

"None." The pack had contained a mass of corbinite; thrity pounds of near-pure crystal worth a half-dozen High Passages together with gear costing most of what he owned. "In the Drell, you say?"

"What? Oh, the boy." Glover sucked in his cheeks as he reached for a bottle. "Join me? No? Well, here's to success." He emptied the glass at a swallow, the reek of crudely distilled spirit tainting the air as he refilled it. "The nearest thing to Lowtown you'll find on Shard. Once it was Lowtown but then the company pulled out and things evened out a little. The poor stayed poor but the top rich got up and went. So what was left was up for grabs." He drank again. "If it hadn't been for my busted foot I'd have gone too. A good job," he said bitterly. "That's what they told me. A good, responsible position. Hell, look at it! Even a Hausi couldn't make a living in this dump!"

A lie—but a Hausi wouldn't have drunk his profits, let his wares rot for lack of attention or wallowed in self-pity.

Dumarest said, patiently, "Where in the Drell?"

"You still on about that boy?" Glover shook his head. "A dumb kid—what's he to you? Have a drink and forget him." He reached for the bottle, halted its movement as he met Dumarest's eyes. "Fivelane," he said. "Number eighteen."

Once it had been smart with clean paint and windows clean and unpatched with paper and sacking. A home with dignity for people with pride. Now it held smells and decay and a slut who stared at Dumarest with calculating eyes.

"Anton," she said. "What do you want with him?" Her expression became speculative. "If you're thinking of—"

"Are you his mother?"

"In a way. His true mother's ill. I can take care of things." She sucked in her breath as Dumarest closed his fingers around her arm. "All right, mister! No harm done! She's upstairs!"

Dumarest found the woman in a room with a narrow window half-blocked with rags against the cold of night. There was a truckle bed, a table, a chair, a box, a heap of assorted fabrics piled in an opposite corner. A jupon of frayed scarlet cloth lay on the lap of a woman who had once been young and could have been beautiful. She coughed and sucked in air to cough again with a betraying liquidity.

"Anton's a good boy," she said. "He does what he can. He wouldn't hurt anyone."

Dumarest was patient. "I mean him no harm. I just want to know about him. Was he born a mute?"

"A genetic defect but it can be corrected. A new larynx—" Her hands closed on the faded scarlet of the patched jupon. "All it needs is money."

The cure for so many ills. Dumarest noted the thinness of the hands, the lankness of the hair. She had met his eyes only at their first meeting, dropping her own as if ashamed, pretending to be engrossed in her sewing. From below came a sudden shout, a slap, a following scream.

"Martia," she said. "Her man has little patience."

"And yours?"

"Dead." Her voice was as dull as her eyes. "Over a year ago now. An accident."

"At work?"

"In the brush. A friend brought the news." She didn't want to talk about it and Dumarest watched the movement of her hands on the jupon. A spare—the garment was edged with gold instead of silver. Anton had not yet returned home. "What do you want, mister?"

"I'm looking for somone. A man named Kelly. He could have been a friend of your husband. Anton might know him. Does he?"

She was silent a moment then she shook her head.

"Think," urged Dumarest. "Your man could have mentioned him. Anton—you can communicate?" He continued as she nodded. "Kelly could have befriended the boy. Jarl too. You know Jarl?"

"No."

Her denial came too fast, perhaps simply an automatic defense. In such places as the Drell strangers were always objects of suspicion and it would be natural for her to protect the boy.

"A pity." Dumarest was casual. "There could be money in

it. I want to get my business done and be on my way. Did your man have a favorite place? Who brought you the news of his death?"

The question was asked without change of tone and she answered with unthinking response. "Fenton. Boyle Fenton. he owns the Barracoon. It's on the corner of Tenlane and Three." She added, "He's a good man."

He had softened the bad news, given her a little money, promised aid if she should need it, a promise she could have been too proud to ask him to keep.

Had the boy been willing bait?

It was possible and he fit the part; young, weak, helpless, unable to do more than jangle his bells, a decoy to disarm the suspicious, placed by the predators who had been willing to kill for what loot they could find. Or had they merely taken advantage of a genuine accident?

"Does Anton go out often?"

"Every day."

"Into the brush? Alone?"

"He's used to it. He collects what he can and sells it for what he can get." Pride in her son lifted the woman's head, a ray of sunlight touching her hair and lending it a transient beauty, echoed in the bones of cheek and jaw, the arched brows over the sunken eyes. The fever staining her cheeks gave her a false appearance of health. "He's a good boy, mister!"

The boy was small and frail and unable to speak yet wise in the dangers of the brush. It had not been an accident, then, but even so he was not wholly to be blamed. Those who had used him carried the guilt.

Downstairs the woman who had greeted him was waiting in the doorway.

"Any luck, mister?" Her eyes moved toward the upper regions. One was dark with a fresh bruise and weals marked the shallow cheek. "If you really want the boy I could arrange it."

Dumarest said, "Is there a hospital here?"

"An infirmary at the Rotunda but they want paying in advance." Her eyes moved over his face to settle on the dried blood marking his lacerated scalp. "For her or yourself? If it's for her then forget it—she won't last another season. If it's for you then why waste money? The monks will treat you for free."

It had been a hard day and Brother Pandion was tired. He rested his shoulders against the sun-warmed brick of the building used as a church and looked at the line which never seemed to end. Many of the faces were familiar; but all were suppliants coming to gain the comfort of confession. They would kneel before the benediction light to ease their guilt, then to suffer subjective penance and, after, to receive the Bread of Forgiveness. And if many came only to get the wafer of concentrates it was a fair exchange—for all who knelt to be hypnotized beneath the swirling glow of the light were conditioned against killing a fellow man.

A fair exchange, but how many would need to be so conditioned before all could walk safely and in peace? Pandion knew the answer, as did all dedicated to serve the Church of Universal Brotherhood, but knowing it did not lessen his resolve. Once all could look at their fellows and recognize the truth of the credo—_there, but for the grace of God, go I!_—the millennium would have arrived.

He would never live to see it as would no monk now living. Men traveled too far and bred too fast yet each person touched by the church lessened pain and anguish by just that amount. Each who saw in another the reflection of what he might have been was a step upward from barbarism and savagery. A life spent in that pursuit was a life well-spent.

He straightened as Dumarest approached, the brown homespun robe shielding the angular lines of his body. Even as a youth he had never been plump and now years of privation had drawn skin taut over bone and shrinking muscle. But the privation had been chosen and was not a duty, for the church did not believe in the virtue of pain or the benefit of suffering, yet how could he indulge himself while so many remained unfed?

"Brother?" His eyes, deep-set beneath prominent brows, studied the tall figure now halted before him. "If you wish to use the church there is a line already waiting." The line was too long and Pandion felt a touch of guilt at his indolence. Brother Lloyd was now on duty, fresh from his time of rest. but even so the guilt remained, tainted, perhaps, by the sin of pride—when would he learn that others could take his place?

He added, "If it is a matter of other business I will be pleased to help."

"A boy," said Dumarest. "A mute about ten years of age. You know him?"

"Anton? Yes."

"He was hurt and I wondered if he'd called here for treatment."

"It is possible," said Pandion. "I have not seen him myself but I have been standing here only a short while. You know him well?"

"No, but I am concerned."

The old monk smiled with genuine pleasure. "He may have asked for help. If so Carina Davaranch would have attended him."

She was tall with cropped hair forming a golden helmet over a rounded skull. Her brows were thick, shadowing deep-set eyes of vivid blue. Her mouth was hard, the lips thin, carrying a determination matched by the jaw. A woman entering her fourth decade yet appearing older than she was. Her hands with their bluntly rounded nails could have belonged to a man.

"You need help?" Her eyes met his own, lifted to the dried blood on his scalp. The dull green smock she wore masked the contours of her body. "You'll have to sit—you're too tall for me to reach."

A man cried out as Dumarest obeyed, pain given vocal expression from a figure stretched on a table to one side and flanked by two others wearing green. Both were males, neither young, monks now busy closing a shallow wound. There was no sign of the boy.

"An accident," she said, noting Dumarest's attention. "A carpenter was careless with a chisel. Now let me look at that head of yours."

He smelt her perfume as she leaned over him and wondered why she had chosen to use it. A defense against the odors natural to such a place? A desire to assert her femininity? Backing, she reached for a swab, wetted it with antiseptic, washed off the dried blood.

"Hold still!" The sting was sharp but quickly over. A spray and it was done. "Just leave it alone for a while and you'll have no trouble. If you can afford to pay for the treatment put it into the box."

A gesture showed where it was. As he fed coins into the slot Dumarest said, "How long have you worked here?"

"I arrived on the *Orchinian* ten days ago. A mistake but I'm stuck with it and I don't like being idle. The monks were willing to let me help."

"Did you treat the boy?"

"The mute? Yes. He has a bruised ankle and minor lacerations but he'll be fine in a few days if he gives it rest." She added, "A pity. A fine boy like that. If he was mine I'd turn harlot if there was no other way to buy him a voice."

"Don't blame her."

"Her?"

"His mother. I've seen her—she's dying."

"I didn't know." Carina looked down at her hands then met Dumarest's eyes again. "Was I so obvious?"

"No." He changed the subject. "What brought you to Shard?"

"I told you—a mistake. I was on Zanthus and two ships stood on the field. I flipped a coin and the odds were against me. Luck, too—I chose the wrong one. Well, thank God I've money to get away from here. And you?"

Dumarest was in trouble unless he found his stolen possessions. Shard had no industry, no easy source of natural wealth. He had been lucky but to live for weeks in the hills required gear and supplies he no longer had. Without money he was stranded and to be stranded was often to starve.

He said, "I'll make out."

"I'm sure you will." Her fingers were deft as she touched his wound. "And maybe you'll learn to duck next time."

"I'll try."

"You do that. No! Wait!" Her fingers held him down as he made to rise. Strong fingers which quested over his skull, the lines of his jaw, lingering on the bones of cheeks and eyebrows. He thought of a surgeon searching for fractures or a sculptor molding a mass of yielding clay. "I'd like to paint you," she said. "Will you sit for me?" She sensed his hesitation. "I'll pay," she added. "It won't be much but I'll pay."

Across the room the man who had cried out rose to sit upright on the edge of the table. He was sweating, his face drawn, haggard. Against the cage of his ribs a broad swath of transparent dressing glistened over the neatly sutured wound.

Looking at him Dumarest said, "Have you treated anyone

today for multiple lacerations? A man, middle-aged, skin torn on the face, back and shoulders."

"No."

"Has anyone else?"

"I've been on duty since dawn." Her fingers fell from his cheek as she stepped back from where he sat. "We've had a woman with a cut lip, a man with two broken fingers, three kids with burns and scalds, a girl who'd swallowed poison. A quiet day. Maybe the infirmary treated the man you're looking for."

"Could you find out?"

For a moment she stared at him then, without comment, left the room. From an annex he heard the blurring of a phone, her voice, a silence, her voice again. Returning, she shook her head. "No."

"Thanks. I owe you a favor."

"You can repay." She loosened the fastening of her smock. "You can take me home."

Chapter Two

Home was a studio set high under peaked eaves, a place bright with windows admitting light which shone on the flaking walls and bare wood on the floor—a loft which held a wide bed, a cabinet, tables, chairs, an easel at which stood the woman and a chair on which Dumarest sat.

It faced the foothills, the tangle of brush now a darker green because of the shifting light, a mass now ominous, menacing, with its hints of lurking dangers. An impression heightened by the dying sun, resting low on the horizon in a sea of umber and orange, russet and burnished copper. An angry sun dying with the speed with which it was born and soon to plunge the world into night.

"Earl! You moved!" Her tone was harsh with genuine anger. "How can I capture your mood unless you hold still?"

A rebuke she had won the right to give and he froze again, eyes searching the brush. Jarl could be lying among the brambles, torn, bleeding, waiting for death. Or he could have found a hole in which to hide until it was safe to return to the town. That safety would come after dark when he would scuttle into a room somewhere to be tended by those with common interests.

But Kelly would be unharmed.

"Earl!"

"Sorry." The pose was awkward and he had held it for too long. "Can I stretch?"

"Later."

She was a martinet but she knew her trade. Her fingers

16

moved with deft grace and her face was lost in the abstract world of a creative artist. A trick of the light turned a pane of the window into a mirror and he watched the tilt and movement of her head, the helmet of burnished hair which framed the strong-boned face. She had changed and now wore a smock which hung loosely from her shoulders, bound at the waist with a scaled belt. A smear of paint on her cheek robbed her of years and she looked somehow young and full of childish enthusiasm.

The illusion was born of mirrors and light and he looked away to search again the brush, the approaches to the town. In the far distance something moved and he tensed, narrowing his eyes, but it was only a scavenger snouting the dirt. He had sat too long and would soon need to be going.

"Now?"

"Now," she said reluctantly. "Come and tell me what you think."

He paused before answering, studying what he saw. The clothing was correct: gray tunic and pants with high boots, the hilt of his knife riding above the right. The background was the same; the foothills beyond the window, the brush, the dying light painting the sky. But the man she had depicted seemed a stranger. The face was a mask fashioned of hate and hurt and a cold determination. A blend swamped by a ruthless savagery which gave him the air of a crouching beast of prey.

"Is that how you see me?"

"That's what I think you are," she corrected. "Not on the surface but way down deep where it matters. A basic animal fighting to survive in the best way it can. The only real difference between you and the rest of us is that you are good at it. Annoyed?"

"No."

"Good." She seemed relieved. "Some men can't stand to see themselves reflected in a true mirror. They strut and pretend to be what they know they are not. Fools who never realize how they display their stupidity."

"Human," said Dumarest. "Human enough not to like their faults and do their best to forget them." He looked again at the painting. "How long did it take you to learn how to do this?"

"To catch the inner mood? Three years. That's how long I

studied at the Brenarch University on Drago. That was before I decided to take up medicine and after I realized I would never be a dancer."

"Drago—your home world?"

"No. I was born on Mevdon. Do you really have sympathy for posturing fools?"

"I try to understand them." He shook his head as he met her eyes. "You work with the monks, Carina—have they taught you nothing?"

"I help the monks," she said. "I can't stand to be bored. But that doesn't mean I believe all they teach. To be tolerant, yes, and to be gentle and kind and have the imagination to be considerate. But I am an artist and to me there is no beauty in dirt and decay, no glory in failure. And, as a doctor, I find nothing but disgust in disease and ignorance."

"A doctor?"

"Five years at the Hamed Foundation on Hyslop. They use hypno-tuition and cellular-experience therapy. I got my degree but I don't claim to be other than mediocre."

He said, dryly, "You must have started young."

"Too damned young!" The bitterness of her reaction surprised him. "I don't know what kind of a childhood you had, Earl, but mine just didn't exist. My father was a genius and wanted me to be the same. So he force-fed me and damned near drove me insane. If he hadn't got himself killed he would have succeeded."

"Your mother?"

"Died at my birth—or so I was told. Sometimes I think I came from a vat. The truth could be that he hired a genetic mate to carry his child and later hired nurses. Anyway, he's dead now. One day I'll go back and dance on his grave."

Dumarest said, "Have you ever been painted by someone as skilled as yourself?"

"No. Why? I—" She broke off, understanding. "The mirror of truth—am I that bad?"

"You're human—just like the rest of us."

"And I pretend just as hard?"

He made no comment but his eyes gave the answer and she frowned, hugging herself, as she looked through the window. Beyond, the world had grown dark, the sun vanishing as if snuffed, and the stars now illuminated the sky with a cold and hostile beauty. Too many stars set too close; the Zaragoza Cluster was a hive of worlds, most similar to Shard—planets which recognized no law and held only the bare elements of civilization. Dead-end worlds, used, discarded, left to scavengers; places devoid of culture and tradition, jungles in which only the strong could hope to survive.

"Night." Carina shivered in the growing cold. "One moment it's summer and then you're smack in the dark of winter. I hate the cold. I was lost once on Camarge; my raft developed a fault and I had to land and wait for rescue. Five days with the temperature never above freezing—hell must be made of ice."

"Camarge," said Dumarest. "You move around."

"So?"

"Three years training to be an artist. Five to be a doctor."

"And I travel." She turned to face him, her eyes bright with defiance. "Now tell me I'm wasting my life."

"I wouldn't say that."

"There are plenty who would. Plenty who have. Settle down, they say. Take care of a man and breed a clutch of children. Be a cook and nurse and bed-mate. Be a real woman." Her tone was brittle with anger. "What do they know about it? A woman's no different from a man in her needs and aspirations. She gets just as restless. The itch to move is just as strong. She gets as stale and as bored as any man ever born."

"So you cut loose," said Dumarest. "Became a traveler."

"Yes," she said. "I travel."

Drifting from world to world, earning her keep as best she could, moving on in a restless search—for what? Peace, she could have said, or happiness, but for her and those like her there could never be either. Always there would be one more world to see, one more passage to take. High if she could afford it with the magic of quicktime to compress hours into seconds. Low if she couldn't, riding doped, frozen and ninety percent dead in caskets designed for the transportation of beasts. Risking the fifteen percent death rate for the sake of cheap travel. And, at the end?

Dumarest had seen them, old, withered, starving on hostile worlds. Not many for few reached old age and fewer were women. They, with a stronger streak of realism, took what they could while still attractive enough to command a degree of security and comfort.

Perhaps Carina would do the same.

The Barracoon was as he'd expected; a room fitted with benches, tables, a bar served by a swarthy, thick-set man with a scarred face. Yellow light from suspended lanterns softened rough outlines and masked the dirt while giving an illusion of warmth and comfort. The floor was torn, stained, the windows meshed with a spider's web of cracks.

Dumarest ordered wine, which was served in a thick mug. Raw stuff with an acrid odor, the product of anything that would ferment.

"I'm looking for Fenton," he said. "Boyle Fenton."

The bartender scowled. "Who wants him?"

"A friend. Send word I'm here." Dumarest looked around and nodded at a table set close to the door. "I'll be over there." He added, "Tell Boyle I don't want to wait too long."

Fenton was a man once hard, the hardness now softened with a layer of fat. His clothing was of good quality, the bulge beneath his jacket warning of a holstered gun. Heavy rings gleamed from his fingers and his eyes matched the gems. He wasted no time.

"I'm Fenton." He sat without invitation, facing Dumarest, one hand poised at the opening of his jacket. "You asked to see me. Why?"

"We have a mutual friend."

"Who?"

"A boy. A mute." Dumarest sipped at the wine. "His name's Anton. You must know him—his father used to hang around here."

"Brill. He's dead."

"So his wife told me. Well, I guess he's no loss. Incidentally she thinks a lot of you. Told me that you were a good man." Dumarest toyed with his mug. "It shows how wrong some people can be."

"Meaning?"

"Nothing. It's none of my business. So what if you did promise to help? A dying woman and a mute kid—what kind of bargain is that?"

He saw the face alter, anger giving life to the eyes, and darted out his left hand to grip Fenton's right as it moved toward the gun hidden under the jacket. Beneath the fat was muscle and Dumarest tightened his grip as Fenton strained.

"You want to carry on with this?" Dumarest kept his voice low as he lifted the mug in his other hand. "Relax or you'll get this in the face." His expression made it no idle threat. "And don't signal to any of your help. If anyone comes close you'll regret it."

"Who the hell are you?"

"No one you need worry about." Dumarest eased his grip as he felt the muscles beneath his fingers relax. Dropping his hand he revealed the welts marking the skin. "All I want is some information. Where can I find the boy?"

"With his mother."

"He isn't there. He must be hiding out somewhere. With a friend, maybe. Someone he knows. You could tell me where to look."

"I'm not sure." Fenton rubbed at his wrist. "I don't see much of him since Brill went. Susan—dying you say?"

"Forget her." Dumarest let irritation edge his voice. "What about the boy? Who was close to his father?"

Anton would have known the man and the places he frequented. Fenton knew of the lad as others would have and they, in turn, would have recognized his value. Some could have used him in the brush.

"She moved," said Fenton abruptly. "Susan, I mean. I offered help but when she didn't ask I figured she was making out. The boy said nothing—how the hell could he? Where can I find her?"

"She's sick," said Dumarest. "Dying, as I told you. Give her a few months and she'll be gone. All you have to do is wait."

"You bastard!"

"Jarl," said Dumarest. "Let's start with Jarl. He knows Anton. Where can I find him?"

"Jarl who?" Fenton shrugged as Dumarest remained silent. "It's a common name. Can you describe him?" He scowled as he listened. "That sounds like it could be Jarl Capron. How the hell did the kid get mixed up with scum like that?"

"Maybe he was lonely. The address?"

"Scorelane. Number seventy-nine. That's all I know."

Scorelane was a slash across town in what had once been

the fashionable quarter. Now the houses looked like raddled old women dressed in rotting finery; windows dull, paint flaking, the whole looking drab and soiled beneath the cold light of the stars. Some places fought back with the use of lights and colored pennons and blaring music; small casinos, eating places, brothels, drug emporiums. Refuges for the optimistic, the hungry, the lonely, the desperate.

Number seventy-nine was a hotel.

"A room? You want a room?" The crone behind the desk looked sharply at Dumarest with faded blue eyes. "That isn't easy to provide at this time of year. We're pretty full and our regulars like to retain their quarters even while working away. But I'll see what can be arranged. You'll pay in advance, of course, and I shall need the highest references."

The woman was lost in illusion, believing the place was what it had never been. Finding escape from reality in a game as she fussed over ledgers she could no longer read.

Dumarest looked beyond her to the wall which held a row of boxes each with a hook for its key. Most were cluttered with assorted debris and all were dusty and grimed.

He said, "I'm looking for Jarl Capron."

"Jarl?" Her face became blank. "You mean Mister Capron?"

"Yes."

"Supervisor Capron?"

"Is he in?" A stupid question; the keys visible belonged to empty rooms. "Which is his room?"

"I can't tell you that!"

"It's important." Truth followed with a facile lie. "I've been sent to collect him and some important papers. An emergency at the workings. Only the supervisor can handle it. The room?"

"Two flights up. Turn right. Number twenty-eight." Her hand went to her mouth. "Be careful not to make too much noise."

An unneeded warning; Dumarest moved like a ghost as he climbed the stairs, keeping to the wall so as to avoid creaking treads. The first flight yielded a dusty landing soiled with dried mud and a wad of crumpled, bloody tissue. A solitary wad and the dirty carpet showed no stains. From behind a door down the passage he heard a woman's voice.

"Hold still, you fool!"

A deeper tone, "That hurts!"

"Serves you right. The next time you come heavy with me I'll take out an eye. Now let me finish fixing that cheek."

The second landing held more dust and a patch of dampness which could have been water spilled from a jug or seepage from a leaking tank. Dumarest skirted it and stepped softly down the length of the passage. A window opened on a narrow metal ladder which in turn ran to the street below. Touching it he felt a crusted dryness and, looking at his hand, saw the brown flakes of dried blood.

Jarl's?

Quietly he stepped back down the passage and halted outside room twenty-eight. The door was scarred, the number blurred, no light showing through the keyhole or beneath the lower edge of the panel. Pressing his ear to the wood, he heard a moaning susurration as of wind in a chimney. Frowning, he stepped back and moved to the head of the stairs as sound came from below. On the lower landing he caught a glimpse of a woman with a man whose cheek was covered with a plaster. He was younger than his companion and bore no resemblance to Jarl. Back at the door of room twenty-eight Dumarest pushed his foot against the door above the lock. A snap and it was open.

Beyond lay darkness broken only by starlight filtering through the uncurtained window. A low moaning. An acrid stench.

Then, suddenly, madness.

It came with a gust of sound and a blur against the pale oblong of the window. A snarling roar as if a beast had broken free and a shape which lunged forward, hands extended like claws, curved to rip and tear, to strike like hammers from the gloom.

Dumarest dropped as something slammed against his temple, breaking open the minor laceration and sending blood to wet his cheek. Stars flashed before his eyes as he rolled, feeling the numbing impact of a hard-driven boot, rolling again as it stamped on the spot where his head had rested. As he rose he knocked aside a clutching hand, ducked to let the other pass over his shoulder, stepped in and drove his fist hard against a solid body. Blow followed blow in quick succession. All driven with the full force of back and shoulders—none seeming to have any effect.

Before him the thing gibbered, roared, flailed at the air, swayed and came in with lowered head and raking feet, rose to spit and tear at Dumarest's scalp and shoulders with jagged shards.

Falling back, he hit the wall beside the door, felt the impact of the switch against his shoulder, threw it to bathe the room in brightness.

Jarl stood blinking at him from before the window.

But Jarl was no longer a man.

The vials lying beside the soiled bed gave the answer; analogues taken to relieve boredom, used now as an anodyne against pain; the compounds used by degenerates addicted to bestial forms. With their aid a man could think himself a snake, a goat, a dog. He would emulate one, act like one, be as unpredictable as any creature of the wild. Jarl had ceased to be human.

He stood like a gorilla, stooped, shoulders hunched, the thorn-ripped parody of his face distorted into a snarling nightmare. In each hand he now held the neck of a broken bottle, the jagged shards reflecting the light in vicious gleams. His mouth was open, slavering, his eyes mere glints between puffed lids. He stank of sweat and rage.

He rushed without warning, hands lifted to raise the crude weapons high. Held like daggers, they swept down to slice the air, missing Dumarest by a fraction as he threw himself to one side. Again, the thing which had been a man moving with the furious speed of a predator, glass opening flesh above Dumarest's ear, shards ripping at the tunic, slicing through the plastic to bare the metal mesh imbedded as a protection in the material.

Before they could strike again, Dumarest had thrown himself clear, coming to rest before the window, steel flashing as he jerked the knife from his boot, metal which glinted with mirror-brightness as he twisted it. He guided it into the creature's eyes, hypnotic, commanding. As they followed the lure he stepped forward, boot lifting, the heel slamming against the jaw. The blow would have knocked an ordinary man unconscious but the surrogate beast only shook its head, snarled, lunged forward in a paroxysm of maniacal fury.

To trip over Dumarest as he dropped before it. To plunge through the window. To be impaled on the railings which stood like rusty spears below.

Chapter Three

———————•◆•———————

"He's dying." Carina was blunt. "You carrying him up here didn't help." She looked disdainfully about the room. "God, what a sty!"

Dirt aggravated by blood, the wreckage of the fight, the whole compounded by his search—which had yielded nothing but items of little value: a gun, some papers, a knife, torn and bloodstained clothing. If Kelly had contacted his partner, he hadn't passed over any of the loot.

"A compliment," she said bitterly. "You leave me to go out and kill a man. All right, so he isn't dead yet, but that's splitting hairs. There's nothing I can do for him. Those railings tore him all to hell inside and you weren't exactly gentle. And why send for me?"

"You're a doctor—or were you lying?"

She said, "One day, maybe, you'll realize just how insulting that question was. Yes, damn you, I'm a doctor and because of that I carry some gear, but only emergency stuff. He needs massive corrective surgery, regrowths, an amniotic tank, months of subjective in slowtime. And before that—oh, to hell with it! What do you want me to do?"

"Make him talk." He met her eyes. "He was in analogue and could still be for all I know. If he is, I want you to snap him out of it and make him conscious and aware. And do it fast—if he's dying as you say then we haven't long."

"Analogue—are you certain?"

For answer he handed her the vials.

"The fool. A double-shot which could blow his mind." She

reached for her bag. "I'll do what I can but you realize the risk?" His eyes told her of the stupidity of the question. "You don't care," she accused. "You don't give a damn if he goes insane or turns into a vegetable. All you want is for him to talk."

"That's right." He looked beyond her at the figure recumbent on the soiled bed. "Now let's stop wasting time."

The door was shut again, held by a chair propped beneath the knob. A barrier against the inquisitive who had thronged the passage and could still be outside. As the woman worked Dumarest looked again at what he'd found. The gun was a copy of that used by the man he had killed, a weapon designed to fire a mass of shot and lethal at short range. He broke it and checked the load, frowning at what he saw.

With his knife he slit the cartridge and tipped the load into his hand.

Not shot as he'd expected but a powder as fine as talc. Fired, it would have thrown a cloud over the area immediately before the gunner and that was about all. The fine dust would have held little kinetic energy and that little would have been quickly lost. It could sting the eyes, perhaps, but little else. Unless it was more than what it seemed.

Dumarest stooped, lifting the powder to his nostrils, taking a cautious sniff. Immediately he lowered his hand and leaned back, fighting the numbing paralysis which had locked his eyes, his jaw, the muscles of his neck. For a moment he felt helpless while the light seemed to revolve with slow deliberation, the glow haloed with glittering rainbows.

Why hadn't Jarl used that instead of the club?

The boy, perhaps? Anton had stood close and the man could have had fears as to the result of the powder fired at one so young. And the other? Both had tried to use clubs— had they thought the loads were more lethal than they really were?

Luck had been with him; had they used the guns he would have been left helpless to freeze in the brush. Had Jarl not used the analogue he could have fired as Dumarest burst into the room. Then, if not before, he would have been willing to kill and there had been no boy to safeguard. No threat to future prosperity.

"Earl!" Carina straightened from the supine figure. "It's going to be close."

"Do your best."

"What I'm doing is killing him."

"He's as good as dead already." Dumarest put aside the gun and picked up the papers. "And unless he talks others might follow him."

Himself, who would be a natural target if Kelly wanted to make himself safe. Anton for fear he might betray his whereabouts. Fenton, even, for having given the address.

The papers held nothing of value; a letter from a woman, a circular, an old notification of dismissal but the reason was closure of the workings and he could not be blamed. The reason why he had taken to haunting the brush, perhaps, but the basic liking for the way of life would have always been present. The desire to hurt, to bully, to rob and terrorize. How many victims had he and his kind left to die.

"Earl!"

The eyes were still bloodshot and the jaw now bore the purple of bruises but the bone was unbroken and the man could talk.

"Bastard! You stinking bastard!" Jarl moved against the torn sheets which held him to the bed. "We should have killed you."

"Where's Kelly?"

"Go to hell!"

Dumarest pushed the woman aside and leaned over the dying man. Light glittered from the knife he lifted, the point slowly descending until it touched the throat.

"Where's Kelly?" The knife pressed harder. "Tell me where to find Kelly!" Harder still, the needle point finding the selected nerve. Carina gasped as Jarl reared in pain.

"God! No! God!"

Dumarest eased the pressure. "Just talk," he said. "Do that and I'll leave you alone. I won't trouble you again and that's a promise. And why protect him? You're hurt and could have died while he's living easy. Why do you think he didn't hand over your share? How do you think I found you?" The knife glittered again as he moved it across the other's field of vision. "All I want to know is how to find him. From you or someone else it's all the same to me." His tone deepened, became feral, "But, for you, man—you'll suffer hell!"

"No!" Sweat ran from the bruised features and the eyes rolled in their sockets. A man in torment from the promptings of his own imagination; the tip of the knife hovered well above his skin. "Dear God, no!"

"Earl!" Carina recoiled at the look he gave her then said, quickly, "Don't be silly, Jarl. Why not talk? Just a few words and it'll be over."

"Stop him!"

"I can't!" The truth and she knew it. "Talk, you fool! Do you think I want you to suffer? Tell him what he wants to know!"

For a moment the bloodshot eyes followed the gleaming menace of the knife, then: "The Durand. He stays at the Durand. Runs a table in part return for bed and board."

"Why work the brush?"

"I don't know. Kicks, I guess. He's smooth." Jarl swallowed, choked, fought for breath. "My guts! God, it hurts!"

"Who was the other man?" Dumarest leaned closer. "Who was he?"

"Berge."

"Anyone else? A lookout?"

"No. I—" Jarl coughed, blood showing at the corners of his mouth. His eyes widened as he sensed the approach of death. "Help me! You promised to help me!"

"How will I know Kelly? What does he look like?" Dumarest snarled his impatience as the man remained silent. "Talk, damn you! Talk!"

Carina said flatly, "He can't. He's dead."

On Shard the Durand was an oasis of culture and refinement maintained by those who could afford the luxury of style; if the glory had long departed, pretense remained.

"My lord! My lady!" An attendant bowed as he extended greetings. "We are honored at your presence. What will be your pleasure? The tables? The restaurant? A spell in scented caverns? Or perhaps you would be interested in a period of contemplation spent in a room designed to cater to varied tastes?"

He paused, waiting, assessing the arrivals with practiced eyes. Dumarest had washed and resealed his wounds but their traces gave him an air of brooding menace. Carina had donned a scarlet gown which somehow accentuated the boyish litheness of her figure. As she turned toward the attendant

Dumarest said, "We'll just have drinks for now. Something long and cool."

They were served in a sheltered alcove by a girl with skin bearing the sheen of oil and eyes which dye and glitter had turned into pools of ancient wisdom. With the drinks came a partitioned tray made of flecked glass, each segment containing a differently colored powder.

"For your pleasure," explained the girl. "The red yields the taste of fire, the brown gives tranquility, the amber exuberance, the green pungency, the yellow creates enticing scents."

"And the blue?"

"For love, my lady."

"An aphrodisiac." Carina shook her head as the girl moved away. "Why do I feel insulted?"

"You shouldn't." Dumarest sipped at his drink. "She gave you fair warning."

"In case you took advantage of me." Carina smiled. "Now I begin to understand. Use it and we might hire a room. I suppose she gets a commission."

A certainty as was the fact that most operating in the hotel would have hired floor space. Dumarest looked at the decorations lining the alcove, all dusty with time and neglect, all needing attention the management couldn't afford to provide.

"Not bad." Carina set down her glass. "A little insipid but I suppose that's what the spices are for. How about food, Earl? Hungry?"

"I can wait."

"I can't. I haven't eaten all day. Shall we try the restaurant?"

"No." His tone ended the matter.

"What then?" Before he could answer she added, "Don't you think it's time you told me what all this is about?"

"You know what it's about. I want to find a man."

"Kelly?"

Probably not his own name; used for the occasion. Without a description he would be difficult to find. Dumarest finished his drink and rose. As Carina moved from the alcove to join him he said, "Move among the tables and check the gamblers. Those playing and those watching as well as the men running the games. Look for scratches on face and neck and hands."

"Jarl said he was running a table."

"Kelly could be acting as a shill. Placing bets and winning by arrangement to encourage the others to plunge. Just check. If you spot anything let me know." He caught her arm as she went to move away. "Don't make it obvious. Just act like a woman out for an evening's fun."

Dumarest watched as she pushed her way into the crowd. She didn't look back, which was good, but she had snatched free her arm as if his hand had burned her flesh. Maybe she just didn't like to be touched. Now he had other things to worry about.

A girl stood to one side selling wrapped portions of stimulating gum. Dumarest smiled as he met her eyes, moved toward her as she smiled in return. Jarl had carried a little money and he dropped some into her tray.

"How's business?"

"The usual."

"Which means it could be better." He selected a portion of gum and held it as he glanced over the salon. "Are all the gamblers here tonight? The regulars, I mean. Those running the tables."

"I think so."

"Could you be sure?" Dumarest added more money to the first. "Please."

She craned her neck then nodded, "As I said. None missing."

"And last night?"

Like the girl who had served the drinks her eyes were painted with dye and glitters. They hardened with sudden suspicion. "What is this, mister?"

"I'm running a check," said Dumarest casually. "If a table's left unworked there's a chance I could move in. If a substitute took over I'd like to know that too. It would help." His smile added to his meaning. "I'd appreciate anything you could tell me." He dropped the portion of gum back into her tray. "Help me now and there could be more later."

For a moment she hesitated, then: "Three tables were closed last night: the cage, the spectrum and the high-low-man-in-between. Lenny runs that one and I know for a fact he was sick. The poker table had a substitute. That's the lot, mister." She smiled as he dropped more coins into her tray. "Thanks—and good luck!"

Lenny was thin, frail, coughing as he called to the crowd. "Place your bets and pick up your winnings. Back high, low or man-in-between. One gets you two. Place your bets, you lucky people. Place your bets."

A simple game with a quick turnover, the odds, as always, with the house. But the thin hands were unscratched and the frail body could never have carried an eighty-pound pack through the brush.

The cage held dice and stood on a layout marked with various combinations and odds. The man running it was gaunt, hollow-chested, gasping for breath as he ran his game. It was poorly attended and Dumarest guessed he would soon be in need of a new pitch.

Spectrum was like poker; seven cards with a double discard, the object being to get one card of each color. Odds were placed on the value of various combinations. The game was favored by those who liked to extend their losses and was not preferred by professional gamblers. It was symptomatic of local conditions that the table was thronged.

The dealer was young and carried plaster on one cheek.

Dumarest looked at him, remembering the couple he had seen back in Jarl's hotel. The same man? If so, where was the woman?

He backed and moved with deliberate casualness among those watching the game. The woman had had dark hair set in tight curls, was as tall as her companion, her skin a soft brown. All he had gained at a fleeting glimpse but he remembered the tone of her voice, its curt harshness. If they had been lovers, why had she objected with such violence? A business association, then, the man her pimp.

Dumarest turned as the dealer looked in his direction. If the man was Kelly he would recognize Dumarest; an advantage Dumarest lacked. Yet if he was, why had he been in the hotel and why the charade to disguise his scratched face?

A trap?

Dumarest considered the possibility as he stood before a mirrored pillar, watching the dealer, the others clustered around the table. Jarl set with the gun loaded with its stunning charge—if he hadn't used the drugs he could have used it to paralyze Dumarest as he came through the door. Had Kelly seen him as he questioned the old woman? Dropped the bloodstained wad of tissue as bait? Hired the woman to talk

at the right moment to provide a neat excuse for the wounded cheek?

Had he been scratched by her fingernails or by thorns?

Reflected in the mirror Dumarest saw the sheen of golden
hair and the warm shimmer of a scarlet gown. As Carina
joined him she said, "Nothing, Earl. Everyone I saw was
clean."

Dumarest said, "The dealer on the spectrum table has a
scratched face. Could you tell if it was done with thorns or
nails?"

"Fingernails? Yes. A thorn would act as a claw and make
a deep and narrow wound. Fingernails would yield a broader
and more shallow wound." She added, "But how will you get
the plaster off for me to see?"

A rip would do it but she would need time to make her examination. To pick a fight would be best. To knock the man
down and bare the cheek and wait for Carina to make her
decision.

"Trail me," he said. "Keep well back as if we were
strangers. When he goes down come in fast—you know what
to do."

Turning from the pillar, Dumarest moved back toward the
spectrum table. The dealer, engrossed, had his eyes on the
cards, the players hoping to win. A moment demanding full
concentration as he gauged the strength of their hands, their
willingness to bluff. A good time to move in.

"Earl!" Dumarest halted as a hand fell on his arm. "Man,
it's good to see you!" It was Emil Zarse, who had traveled to
Shard on the same ship. He was an entrepreneur interested in
seeing what could be gained from the abandoned workings, a
wisp of a man with a seamed and wrinkled face now express-
ing genuine regret. "Too bad what happened, Earl. I told you
you'd be better off coming in with me. How long were you
out there? Three weeks—and to lose it all."

Dumarest said, "How did you know I'd been robbed?"

"He told me." Zarse glanced toward the poker table, indicated the man who stood in the dealer's place. "Ca Lee."

Ca Lee was big and bland with slanted eyes and a thick
mass of dark hair neatly arranged in a series of curls—a man
with a decadent air; someone who would take pleasure in another's pain. His hands were deft as he dealt the cards, his
voice a warmly feral purr as he droned the results.

"A lady, no help. A ten to make a pair. A deuce to match two others. A lord, no help. A seven, no help. Deuces to bet."

Seven-card stud and the holder of the three deuces, a woman, trembled in her eagerness to ride her luck. The last card had yet to be played but Dumarest guessed she had another pair hidden. Guessed too that Ca Lee would hold the better hand.

Ca Lee—Kelly, the man's ego had made him reluctant to do more than distort his name.

He looked up as Dumarest edged forward, the slanted eyes widening a little even as the thin lips lifted at the corners in derisive mirth.

"You wish to take a hand, friend?"

"I can't afford it."

"No? Then make room for those who can."

Dumarest said, "I'll go when you answer a question—how did you know I'd been robbed?"

The cards stilled in the deft hands then, as the man smiled, resumed their soft rippling. "You're Dumarest," he said. "The one I've heard about. Too bad about what happened."

"Who told you?"

"I heard it from someone." The shrug was expressive. "You know how talk gets around."

"From Berge? He died. Jarl Capron? He was too badly hurt to gossip. Mel Glover? He didn't know. Who, Ca Lee? Who told you?"

"Someone. I forget. The boy, perhaps."

"A mute?" Dumarest heard the soft rustling as those standing close moved away, sensing the tension, the rising anger. "I told no one—and how did you know the boy was involved?"

A mistake and the man's eyes changed as he realized how he'd betrayed himself. A change followed by immediate action as he threw the deck of cards.

They left his hand in a fan, spinning, a collection of paper-thin knives aimed directly at Dumarest's eyes. Sharp edges which would cut and blind like a handful of steel. Dumarest ducked, felt them glance from his hair, dropped lower to the floor and lunged for the legs he saw on the far side of the table.

Ca Lee was fast and he had friends.

As Dumarest rolled after the retreating legs a foot appeared to send its toe driving into his ribs. Another stamped at his groin, missing, as he rolled. He screamed as, gripping the foot, Dumarest rose, twisting, throwing him back to land with a dislocated hip. As his companion came in, punching, Dumarest spun, stabbed with stiffened fingers, sent the man to fall, vomiting blood from a ruptured larynx.

Halfway across the room Ca Lee raced toward a door.

"Earl!" Carina's voice was shrill with warning. "To your right!"

A man armed with a croupier's rake missed as, far too late, he slashed at Dumarest's head, but he lost his determination as he saw his intended victim's face. As he retreated, Dumarest reached the door through which Ca Lee had vanished.

It led to a passage running to either side, flanked with doors, dimly lit, with pools of shadow lying in pillared alcoves. Dumarest halted, hearing the pad of running feet and turned left to follow. A junction, a startled girl looking after a fleeting shape, then a bend and stairs rising in a tight spiral to the upper levels. If Ca Lee was hurrying to his room he would have taken them but Dumarest slowed with the instinctive caution of a hunter. A trail made too obvious could lead to a dead end or a lethal trap. He moved on, found other stairs leading below, knelt to rest his ear against the metal treads. A thrum and quiver of distant vibration and he rose to follow it, emerging in a shadowed, cavernous dimness laced with pipes and conduits, redolent with a variety of smells.

The basement of the Durand, the pipes serving the various facilities: steam and water for the sauna and pool, wires with power for lights and heating plates. In the shadows something moved.

Dumarest tensed, knife lifted to throw, the cast halted as he recognized the source. A rat scuttled across his path to vanish into shadow. But what had made it run?

He backed, blending into darkness, moving with soft caution, careful as to where he set his feet. A few yards and he sensed rather than felt an obstruction to his rear. He sidled around a massive tank, his ears strained, eyes narrowed for sound and movement.

He heard a sighing sound, another repeated from a point yards distant to one side—the escape of steam or the faint exhalation from human lungs? Dumarest reached into a pocket and found a coin. With his left hand he flipped it to one side, hearing it fall, seeing a blur of movement and springing forward, he lifted the knife.

And heard the sudden jangle of bells.

He dropped, rolling, as the narrow ruby guide-beam of a laser slashed the air where he had stood. The burning lance created a patch of flame to the accompaniment of harsh jangling. A shot followed a curse as Ca Lee sprang forward, the laser moving in his hand, the barrel slanting to aim at where Dumarest lay.

To fall as steel spun glittering through th air, the point of the knife finding the face, an eye, driving into the brain beneath.

Chapter Four

The scarlet gown was marred with ugly smears of darker hue staining the fabric, blood which had dried as she worked. Now, straightening, Carina wiped her forehead with the back of her hand, careless of the trail she left behind.

Dumarest was impatient. "Well?"

"He'll live," she said. "The beam charred bone but missed vital organs. I've fixed the seared tissue and administered prophylactic therapy together with hormone healing compounds. That's all I can do with what I've got."

"How long?"

"Until he's up and running? About a month. A pity we can't use slowtime."

It would heal him in a day but was expensive and, while effective, gave rise to complications. The accelerated metabolism demanded a continuous intake of energy if tissue-deterioration was to be avoided. Looking at the lad's frail body Dumarest knew he lacked the resources to take advantage of the drug. Too little fat, too little strength in reserve. To give it would be to kill.

"See that he gets the best available," he said. "What you haven't got, buy from the infirmary. I'll pay."

"Conscience money?"

"I didn't burn him."

"But it was because of you he got hurt." Her voice was sharp with accusation. "Three men dead," she said bitterly. "A boy almost killed and for what? Because you'd been robbed. Because you wanted your goods back. For money!"

36

His actions seemed dictated by greed or pride, but she knew it was more than that. It was a matter of survival, rather, his reaction a conditioned reflex born of a time when to be robbed was to be threatened with starvation, when each scrap of food became associated with continued existence and a thief was tantamount to a murderer. The association continued and she wondered what kind of childhood he had known.

Looking at him, seeing the hardness of his face, she knew it couldn't have been easy.

"I'm sorry," she said. "That was a stupid thing to have said. I guess seeing him lying there, working on him——" She broke off, then said angrily, "What the hell was he doing in the basement anyway?"

Scavenging, trying to keep warm, to stay out of sight. Surviving in the best way he could. Dumarest could understand that. Turning from the small figure on the couch, he looked around the dispensary. Little had changed. To one side a monk murmured comfort to a woman as he extracted shards of glass from a lacerated cheek—the result of a quarrel with a professional rival. A man sat on a bench with his throat bandaged, staring at the floor, a failed suicide who would speak in whispers from now on if he was able to speak at all. He didn't look up as Brother Pandion entered the room and made his way to where Dumarest was standing.

"Good news," he said. "I've seen Anton's mother. She was, I'm happy to say, not alone. Her friend——"

Carina was sharp. "A man?"

"Boyle Fenton. An old associate of her husband's. There seems to have been some romantic liaison between them in the past and he is most concerned as to her welfare. And there was a promise made of which he was reminded." The monk glanced at Dumarest. "A happy event. Fortunately she can be cured. Fenton has agreed to meet the expense but his funds are limited and——"

"The boy is my concern," said Dumarest. "I'll take care of that."

Pandion bowed. "You are most kind, brother. We do what we can but our resources are limited."

All he had was consolation and the use of hypnotic techniques to ease the torment of the sick and dying, salves to heal sores and ulcers, antibiotics to alleviate disease. Most of all the comfort and warmth of human sympathy.

Outside the day had grown warm with the sun well above the horizon and Dumarest was conscious of his fatigue. It gritted his eyes and made the pack he'd recovered from Ca Lee's room heavier than it was but before he could rest there were still things needing to be done.

Glover looked up as he entered the store, nodding a greeting as he reached for a bottle, one foot dragging as he moved.

"Have a drink, Earl. I figure you deserve it after last night." The wine was a pale amber, sweet, holding an unexpected bouquet. "Bramble-flower," he explained. "I've more brewing from frond-bloom but it isn't ready yet." He sobered, looking into his glass. "I heard about the boy. Will he be all right?"

"He was lucky."

"No permanent injuries? I mean—"

"I said he was lucky." Dumarest sipped a little of the wine. Over the rim of the glass Glover's face looked strained, his eyes anxious. "He'll heal as good as new."

"I'm glad." Glover sounded sincere. "He's had a bad enough time without those scum making it worse. Jarl I can understand, Berge too—both losers and desperate—but what made Ca Lee do it? He was living soft enough." He drank and refilled his glass. "At least he could walk without dragging a leg."

"So could you."

"Sure, with surgery and money to pay for it. I could even find a decent woman . . . hell, while we're dreaming let's go all the way." Glover swayed a little—the bottle wasn't his first. "The kind of woman a man dreams about. One to make him wish he was young and whole and rich enough to afford what she has to offer." He drank again and stared into the empty glass and then slammed it down and threw back his shoulders. Later, drugs would provide a dream surrogate of what he yearned to possess and he would wake filled with a vague despondency. An emptiness to be filled with more drink, more drugs. "You come to trade, Earl?"

"That's right." Dumarest dumped his pack on the counter. "What will you offer for this?"

As Glover made his examination Dumarest wandered

about the store. Little had changed; the baskets stood as he
remembered, the jars and pots, the bales and bundles. The
bench beneath the window still held a book and the binoculars. Dumarest picked them up and lifted them to his eyes.
Before him the brush jumped to magnified enlargement.

"A hobby," said Glover, noticing. "With this leg of mine
it's hard to get around. When I'm not busy I like to look at
the hills. See Anton at work, maybe."

"A hobby? Like brewing wine?"

"Just things to do." Glover looked at the stuff he had
spread on the counter. The mass of corbinite stood bright
among the rest. "The camping and survival gear isn't worth a
lot, but the corbinite is in fair demand. I'll offer——" He broke
off as Dumarest rested his hand on his arm. "Something
wrong?"

"I just don't want you to be too hasty," said Dumarest.
"You've seen the stuff, now let's talk a little. About your hob-
bies," he added. "About people you know. Berge, for example."

"I don't know anything about him!"

"Of course not." Dumarest smiled without humor. "But
you know he's dead. You might even know how he died."

Glover, sweating, licked his lips.

"A man like you," said Dumarest. "One foot dragging and
thinking of his bad luck all the time. Dreaming of the women
he'd like to own and the things money could buy. A man
with a store and a powerful pair of binoculars and plenty of
time to use them. One who could talk to a mute, maybe, with
signs and expressions. Do you see what I'm getting at?"

"Earl! I swear——"

"I could have died." Dumarest was harsh. "Been killed in
the brush. Been killed again by Jarl. Again by Ca Lee. Three
dead—maybe it should be four?"

"No!" Glover shook his head, eyes wide with fear. "You're
wrong, Earl. I. . . . No, Earl! No!"

"You seem to get my meaning." Dumarest lifted his hand
and glanced at the items spread on the counter. "I'm glad of
that. Now let's talk about how much you're going to give me
for my stuff."

Carina said, "You robbed him, Earl. Why else should he
have given you so much?"

"He wanted to."

"I'd like to know why." She leaned back in her chair, hair a glistening helmet, lips paled by the scarlet of her newly cleaned gown. "Did you threaten to kill him?"

"No."

The truth was that Glover's own conscience had made him the victim of his guilt. There was his lack of curiosity when Dumarest had returned after three weeks of prospecting without even a pack. His knowledge of Berge's death when the man still lay where he had fallen in the brush.

"But you suspected him?"

"He had to be involved," he said. "For the usual reason, of course. Greed."

"But you let him buy his life. Why?" She answered her own question. "For money. For Anton to get his chance. Dead he would be of no help at all. And I can imagine how glad he was to get out of it so easily. If you looked like you did when you chased Ca Lee he would have jumped at the chance. How you fought—I've never seen anyone move so quickly. At times you were just a blur." She took a sip of the wine standing before her and added, "Why didn't you tell me?"

"That I had been robbed?"

"It would have helped. When you questioned Jarl I took you for a sadist."

Dumarest said, "You couldn't talk about what you didn't know."

"So the man who knew had to be guilty." She nodded, understanding. "Ca Lee was a fool. There was no need for him to have left his table the previous night."

A mistake he didn't correct; the man would have needed time to get into position and would have wanted the cover of darkness to shield him from prying eyes.

"He underestimates you," she said. "Any other man would have complained. Talked about his loss. Tried to get help. You know, Earl, you are no ordinary man."

And she seemed no ordinary woman. He watched as she leaned back and sipped again at her wine. They had eaten and were now surrounded by the decaying luxury of the Durand, lingering over a dish of sweetmeats and a bottle of wine. Dumarest felt relaxed now that he had eaten but fatigue still gritted his eyes. The days were short on Shard as were the nights but he had been awake since his last camp in the hills. Carina also must be tired but she seemed as fresh as ever. Was that due to drugs or a naturally efficient metabolism which rid her body of toxic wastes?

"It's natural," she said when, bluntly, he asked. "A genetic trait. I only need half the sleep of a normal person."

"Convenient."

"At times, yes," she admitted. "At others it isn't so pleasant. The time can drag when everyone is asleep and thought's your only companion. But it helped when I was studying."

"And when you were a child?"

"I dreamed. I lay with my eyes wide open staring at the ceiling and I dreamed of castles in the sky and great beasts and armies which would fight for me and magicians who would perform wonders at my command. I dreamed of vast and empty lands and long and endless journeys." She drank the last of her wine. "I dreamed of nothing but escape."

"And now?"

"I don't know," she confessed. "To move on, I guess. To find new places."

"To look for the one place which will mean happiness," he said gently. "To search for that illusive something which will make you forget the terrors of childhood and fill your days with an assortment of joys."

"To find Bonanza," she whispered, responding, continuing the game. "Heaven or El Dorado. Jackpot or even Earth." She laughed and picked up her glass and shook her head on finding it empty. Dumarest gave her half his own and they faced each other, glass in hand as if about to make a toast. She turned the accident into determination. "To all the hopes that ever were, Earl. To all the planets which can never be. To myths and legends and worlds born of imagination. To you, to them, I drink!"

He followed her example, draining the bottle into their glasses as she lowered her own, giving her the lion's share. Accumulated fatigue must, by now, be dulling the sharp edge of her mind and the extra alcohol would help to loosen her tongue. She had mentioned Earth. She was a traveler and she had mentioned Earth!

Then he realized his own fatigue had bolstered false hopes. She had mentioned Earth but only in passing and with others

accepted to be legends. To her as to others Earth was as un-
real as the dream of an eternal paradise or a world made of
solid diamond. No almanac listed it. No navigational tables
held its coordinates. No one he had ever met admitted it
could be real.

But Earth existed—he was living proof of that. He had
been born on that lost and forgotten world. One day, he
would find it again.

The studio was as he remembered: the table, the bed, the
paintings stacked against a wall. He closed the door and
jammed a chair beneath the knob, then turned to meet her
wide, watchful eyes.

"I'm staying," he said. "A precaution." He saw her glance
toward the bed, sensed her trepidation and added quickly,
"Ca Lee could have had friends. Some of them might not like
the way he died."

"But you killed him!"

"And you're easier to hurt." He remembered the woman in
the dispensary with her lacerated face and put a snap into his
voice. "Don't argue about it. Just go to bed—I'll take the
chair."

She was like an animal, lying wakeful and tense and he
wondered why. The way she had snatched her arm free of his
grasp held a clue and he wondered what had been done to
her to induce such fear. Or was it a fear of inner weakness?
A need to which she dared not succumb? The questions
ceased to have meaning as fatigue weighted his eyelids and
drove him into restless sleep . . . broken as the woman
moved.

"Earl?" She looked at his hand as he gripped her wrist,
face ghostly in the starlight streaming through the window.
"Please, Earl! Please!"

"You startled me." He released her hand. "You shouldn't
have come so close to me." He rubbed his eyes, the sleep,
though short, had removed some of the grit. "Have you
water?"

She gave it to him in a cup, pouring from a pot damp with
moisture which she took from a recess in the wall. He sipped
and tasted a faint salinity. Had hers been a hot and arid
world?"

"No," she said when he asked. There are mountains and

seas and fertile land and everything is clean and bright as if it were new. You'd never see a cripple in the streets and no one would have to live as Anton does." Pausing, she asked, "Why, Earl? Why spend what you did on his welfare?"

"Bells."

"What?"

"Bells," he said again. "They warned me. Down in the basement when I hunted Ca Lee. I saw Anton move and thought he was the man I was after and sprang forward—"

"And would have killed him if you hadn't heard the bells." She nodded, understanding. "Then Ca Lee would have had you at his mercy. But were you kind only to repay a debt?"

A boy, handicapped, fighting to survive in a hostile environment, Anton could have been himself. Dumarest rose from the chair and stepped toward the window to look at the stars, the slope of the foothills now dark and solid in the silver light. A boy's hunting ground—his own had been far less gentle—but no child should have to creep among thorns to harvest a little fruit.

Turning, he said to lighten his thoughts, "Tell me about your home. What color are the seas? The sky? Do you have a moon?"

"Green," she said. "And azure and, yes, we do have a moon. Two of them in fact but one is very small. At times it glows scarlet."

"Bad times?" He saw the movement of her eyes, the tensing of small muscles in her face and took another sip of water, knowing he had touched a sensitive area. "Why don't you go back to bed?"

"I couldn't sleep. The bed's yours if you want it."

"Later, perhaps." His nerves were too edgy to permit of deep and restful sleep and it would be better for him to stay awake. Dumarest drank the rest of the water and set down the cup. It fell to the floor, and as he picked it up his hand brushed the edge of the stacked paintings. "You've been busy," he commented. "May I see them?"

"Why not?" She snapped on the light and lifted them and set them on the table face upwards. "I'll have to make a decision about them soon."

"Too many?"

"Too heavy. I like to stay mobile."

He nodded and looked at the paintings. Each was on a thin

sheet of metallized paper and could be flexed and rolled without damage. Final products; the one she had made of himself had been crude by comparison. She guessed what he was thinking.

"I was in a hurry but I'd like to paint you again. I'd be able to achieve greater depth this time now that I know you better. What do you think of that?"

A rose lay on a cushion, the petals dewed, the stem with its spines so real that he could almost smell the perfume.

"And that?"

An egg, broken, the bird newly hatched, struggling with tiny wings to free itself from the smooth prison. Each feather was a fluffed gem. The gaping beak seemed to be sounding all the fury of all the creatures ever born. The eyes held in their orbits the panoply of worlds.

"And these?"

Dumarest leafed through them, pausing to look at the woman. "Did your father ever see any similar work?"

"Of mine? No."

"A pity. If he had he wouldn't have died a disappointed man."

Frowning, she said, "I don't understand, Earl."

"He wanted you to be a genius, you said." Dumarest touched the painting in his hand. "This is proof of it. The proof of his success—your success. I—" He broke off, looking at the next to be revealed.

A woman, seated on a casket, and she was old.

Old!

The accumulated weight of years piled invisible mountains on her shoulders, bowing them, hollowing the thin chest to match the hollows of her cheeks, the sunken pits in which dwelt her eyes. Her hair was a cloud of whiteness holding the fragile delicacy of gossamer. The hands resting on her lap were brittle straws ending pipestem arms which matched the reed-like figure. The face was creped with a countless mesh of lines, the lips thin and bloodless, the whole giving the impression of a mask.

Old!

Old—and patient.

The impression was almost tangible and dominated the portrayal. The woman was old and yet not ugly. She held the same beauty as a tree that is old or a lichened wall or the worn hills of ancient worlds. The mask-like face looked at things created by time beyond normal comprehension—the span of years which had passed in a ceaseless flow from the time of her conception and would continue long after she was dust. Time spent in waiting as she was waiting now. Waiting with the incredible patience of the very old.

"Who—?"

"She isn't real," said Carina, anticipating his question. "Not an actual person. She symbolizes an ideal."

Age and patience and waiting—but waiting for what?

Dumarest closed his eyes, pressed the lids tightly together, looked again at the timeless face of the old woman. An ideal, Carina had said. An artist's impression—but of what?

"The box," she said when he asked. "I saw it and was curious and made some inquiries. It looks like a shipping container but it isn't that and neither is it a coffin. I thought it was at first, despite its size, but I was wrong. It's the reverse, in fact. A survival-casket."

That was new to him. Ships carried life-support sacs for use in emergency but they were a last hope and a desperate gamble. The usual caskets were strictly functional affairs shaped by the need to achieve a low temperature in the minimum time and to keep it stable once obtained. And why the old woman? The impression of limitless patience?

"They wait," said Carina. "Those who use the boxes, I mean. I depicted an old woman but it could have been a man. And I guess neither had to be old but that's how I felt it. Old people lying in their boxes in a form of suspended animation while the years spin past outside. Just lying there, waiting. Patiently waiting."

"For what?"

She shrugged, indifferent. "Who knows? They are crazy, of course, they have to be. To waste a life just lying in a box in the hope you'll be able to last long enough to be around when whatever you're waiting for happens. The end of the universe, maybe. The discovery of immortality. Who knows?"

And who cared? Oddities were common in a galaxy thick with scattered worlds bearing a host of varying cultures. Societies with peculiar beliefs and customs strange to any not of their kind. Frameworks of reference which turned madness into normal behavior. Freaks and fanatics going their own way, tolerated or ignored as long as they did no harm.

Dumarest put down the painting, half-turned, then reached for it again with belated recognition. The woman dominated the scene or he would have noticed it before. Had noticed it but fatigue had delayed his reaction. Now he studied the painting again, concentrating, not on the woman but on the box.

It was decorated with a profusion of painted symbols.

"Earl?" He turned and saw her face, the anxiety in her eyes, and realized he had stood silent and immobile for too long. "Earl, is anything wrong?"

"No. Where did you see this?"

"The box? Why, Earl, is it important?"

"Where!"

"On Caval," she said quickly. "The Hurich Complex—Earl, please!"

He turned from her, smoothing his face, forcing himself to be calm. She didn't know. She couldn't know—to her the box was nothing more than an oversized sarcophagus. An amusing novelty which had triggered her creative artistry. The symbols adorning the casket merely vague abstractions.

Symbols which could guide him to Earth.

Chapter Five

Caval rested on the edge of the Zaragoza Cluster, a small, fair world of balmy air and rolling fields, devoid of the stench of industrial waste, the bleak shapes of functional machines; a world in which time seemed to have slowed, even the clouds drifting with stately grace across the pale amber of the sky. The people matched their world, adapted and conditioned by inclination and environment: slow, stolid, a little bovine but far from stupid.

The Hurich Complex lay thirty miles from the landing field on the far side of a ridge of rounded hills now bright with yellow flowers which covered crests and slopes with a golden haze. The place itself was wrapped in the easy somnolence of a tranquil village; wide streets flanked by open-fronted shops in which craftsmen plied their trade. The air carried the endless tap of hammers, the scuff of files, the echoes of saws and planes. The place was a hive of industry devoid of the mechanical yammer of machines—all work was done by hand.

"There!" Carina lifted a hand, pointing. "It was down that street, I think. Yes, it was down there—I recognize the sign over that shop."

A swinging plaque bore the imprint of a rearing beast adorned with a crown—carved wood touched with gilt and paint bearing a startling likeness to a living creature. The street itself was given to residential establishments, only a few of the houses with the familiar open front, some closed with broad windows displaying the goods within.

"On the left," said Carina. "About halfway down."

She had insisted on accompanying him as a guide when he had left Shard. Now she walked three paces ahead of him as if eager to prove her memory correct. She wore the slacks and tunic she had donned when leaving Shard: loose fabric of dull green which disguised her femininity: Her boots were high but soft, the belt wide and fitted with pouches. She carried no visible weapons.

"Here!" She halted and looked to either side, frowning. "I'm sure it was here. Over there, I think."

Dumarest looked at a blank wall.

"I'm sorry, Earl. I'm sure it was there."

He said, "When you left here did you go straight to Shard?"

"No. I shipped to Mykal and moved around a little. I did the painting there and worked in the local hospital for a while. Then I got bored and went to the field and tossed a coin and moved on."

To Shard, and more time had been spent on the return voyage. Time enough for the shop to have closed, the owner to have died.

Had he arrived too late?

The sign of the rearing beast had denoted a tavern, and, in a long, cool room adorned with masks and weapons all carved from wood, the owner served beer and nodded in answer to Dumarest's inquiry.

"The shop down the street? Jole Nisbet sold it about a month ago. Young Zeal's taken it and should do well. A fine worker in glass and ceramics. He'll be open in a couple of weeks if you're interested."

"Nisbet?"

"To another shop, of course. It's on Endaven. . . . Turn right at the junction and it's three hundred yards down."

They came to a big, bustling place filled with the scent of wood and resin and paint, littered with shavings and dust and scraps of metal. Jole Nisbet, old and gnarled, with the strength of a tree, looked at Dumarest, then at Carina. For a long moment he said nothing, then smiled.

"The artist. You are the artist—am I right?" He beamed as she nodded. "And you've come back to us and with a friend. I hope you will stay. We need such talent as yours."

"Thank you, Jole."

"And you?" The shrewd eyes met Dumarest's. "Not an artist, I think, though I could be wrong. A hunter? A farmer? No, your eyes are too restless. A hunter, then—but what else?"

"A student," said Dumarest.

"Of what? War?" The old man shook his head. "We have no place for such a thing here on Caval. A man is born and he works and develops his skills and he lives at peace. He has pride in what he has made or what he does for not all can create things of beauty. Even so someone must sweep the shop and sharpen the tools and carry the timber—no man need consider himself a failure."

A philosophy with obvious results. Since landing on Caval Dumarest had seen no beggars, no signs of abject poverty. Work and pride in work united all in a common bond. Ambition lay in producing something others would admire and their praise was reward enough. And a clean floor could be admired as sincerely as a carved statue, a well-cooked meal as much as any fabrication of metal.

Carina said, "The last time I was here I saw a box in your old shop. I asked about it, remember?" She continued as the old man nodded. "My companion is interested in it."

"Why?"

Dumarest said, "I told you I was a student. It poses a mystery to me which you could answer."

"Why anyone should want to stretch their life-span at the cost of living?" Nisbet shook his head. "I can't help you. I don't know. To be cooped is always bad but to spend a life in sleep and dreams—" He broke off, shaking his head. "Why anyone should do that is beyond me. You must find your answer somewhere else."

He had jumped to the wrong assumption but Dumarest didn't correct him. Instead, he said, "Who could that person be? The owner of the box?"

"Perhaps."

"Who would that person be?" In a moment Dumarest recognized the mistake he had made. "I apologize," he said quickly. "The question could have been misunderstood. It was badly phrased. I was not, of course, asking you to divulge a confidential matter." His tone lowered a little. "As an intruder into your life I ask your tolerance for any unwitting errors I may make or insults I may tender as the result of my ignorance. Of your charity I beg that you take no offense where none is intended."

The old man relaxed beneath the formal intonation. Politeness, in his culture, ranked with deference to acknowledged skills and the respect due to age.

"Confidence must be respected," he said. "Even if only implied. Now, as to the box, some things I can tell you for they are common knowledge. The contents, for one, though they could be varied aside from the essential basics. We are actually at work on one now. If you would care to see it?"

He led the way into a back room where the casket stood supported on stands in the center of the floor. Men were busy at work within the interior, soft scrapings coming from beneath their hands, small tappings, rasps, the sound of abrasions. They rose and stepped back at the old man's command and Dumarest looked at the product of their labors.

The carvings were incomplete as yet but recognizable. A row of tiny depictions ran around the upper surface of the interior—animals, birds, people, fish, insects—a gamut of life-forms, each image a potential gem. The artistry converted something hard and cold and efficient into something no less efficient but far more pleasing.

As yet the outside was untouched, smooth surfaces bearing a soft sheen. The lack seemed to make the container larger and uglier than the one Carina had depicted. Perhaps she had distorted its true dimensions to achieve an artistic symmetry. Dumarest measured it with his eyes: twelve feet long, half as much high and wide. Huge for a coffin, large even for a sarcophagus, but small for a miniature world.

"The outside?"

"Will be decorated in due time."

"According to instruction?"

"Naturally." Nisbet lifted his head as the deep notes of a bell echoed from somewhere outside. "The evening bell and the time of relaxation."

"About the decorations," said Dumarest. He raised his voice against the bustle of noise as craftsmen rose and stretched and put aside their tools. "Could you—"

"Later," said Nisbet. He was curt though his tone remained polite. "For today, work is over. Come again tomorrow."

The tavern provided accommodation as it provided a meal.

Dumarest sat with Carina in the long, low-roofed chamber and ate succulent vegetables served with tangy sauces and a variety of nuts. A dish between them held livers of meat roasted and spiced and set on long skewers. The bread was rough but pleasingly flavored. The wine the same.

"Nice." Carina leaned back and sighed with enjoyment. "At times, Earl, everything seems to be just right. This place, the food, the atmosphere—it's what they mean when they talk of perfection."

"Who?"

"All those who've never had it but have imagination enough to guess what it must be like." She sobered a little. "Of course the right company helps."

He said nothing, looking through the window toward the hills, dusted with gloom now but still bright with their golden mantle.

"In a few weeks the ships will come," she said as if reading his mind. "The blooms will be near-venting then and, when they open, the air will be a cloud of spores and perfume. Golden spores in a scented mist." Her eyes, her voice, held the fascination of a dream. "A time of wonder, Earl, when reality yields to magic and all things are possible. Love, friendship, companionship." Her hand reached out to rest fingers on his own. "That, I think, is the most important. To be close to someone on equal terms. To share his life yet to remain an individual. Something a wife can never do."

"Or a lover?"

"What is love? A man says he loves you and what he really means is that he wants you to love him. For some, it seems, it is enough but there is so much more. To stand beside someone, to be important to him, to be a comrade, a friend." Carina shook her head and sipped at her wine, then, apparently casual, changed the subject. "What do you think of life here?"

"It goes on."

"But better than most. To sit and create a thing of beauty for its own sake and the pleasure of doing it. To sell it or not as you please. A man could work for a year and set his work in a window and wait for someone to offer something he is willing to take in exchange."

"Money."

"No, Earl, not always. That's what I like about this

world—they are not contaminated by greed. And they are right. Money isn't everything. There are so many things it can't buy."

He said, smiling, "Name three."

"You're a cynic."

"Name them!"

She responded to his challenge. "Happiness, honesty, health."

"How about truth?"

"Truth?" She picked up a scrap of bread and crumpled it between her fingers, not meeting his eyes, her own fastened on the dusty hills. "A thing to be searched for and not often to be found. Still less to be recognized when it is. Always to be hated when revealed. Truth is reality. Dreams shield us from it."

As the boxes shielded those who used them. Dumarest looked at the window; her face was dimly reflected in the pane. Like these people Carina had built defenses against a universe not to her liking. Did she travel to find one she could accept?

Gently he said, "Why don't you stay here? As an artist you would be welcome. You could make a home here for yourself. A place to call your own."

"I could," she admitted, and turned to face him. "I've thought about it and been tempted. My work on display for those who come to look and examine and buy. But I'm a creator, Earl. I need stimulation—what did you think of Nisbet?"

He sensed her meaning. "Old and rigid in his ways."

"A stickler for tradition and this world is full of others like him. It's a good world, Earl, a kind one, but the price you pay to enjoy living here is to yield your independence of thought and imagination. To stop wanting to know what is over the next hill. To live by the sound of a bell."

The curfew at dusk and morning signaled the time to eat, sonorous echoes which punctuated the hours of existence.

The echoes to Dumarest would have been the bars of a cage. He said, "Stay here and finish your wine. I'm going to take a walk outside."

He stepped with long strides away from the building, heading west down the main street, taking the next left and then another. He slowed as he neared the corner forming the last side of the square he had traversed, halting at the junction to look at the tavern. Carina was nowhere in sight and he moved up the street to examine the blank wall where Nisbet's old shop had stood. The mortar was almost new, dry but unstained by weather. The place itself held half the capacity of his new premises.

In the street where they had stood he walked slowly past, pausing to casually scan the area. The shop was closed with heavy shutters, the door to one side leading, he guessed, to the upstairs quarters, open to reveal a flight of wooden stairs. An inner door set into the wall would give access to the shop, but, like the shutters, it was closed.

Dumarest walked to the end of the street and back up the one beyond so as to study the premises from the rear. The dying sunlight tinted the upper windows with a golden haze, touching the summit of the rear wall which circled a yard with amber sheens. The low wall could be easily climbed and was devoid of spikes or shards of protective glass. The offices would be to the rear of the workshops and so would open on the yard as did the large assembly area inside, as he had noticed. Unless workers lived within the shop itself the place would be deserted after the curfew bell had sent all to their beds.

Dumarest walked on, thinking about the box Carina had painted, the one he had seen within the shop—small environments which could be sealed against the outside universe. Equipped with food, water, drugs, air—everything needed. Equipped, too, with antigrav units for easy handling, its own power source, an electronic shield which made it impossible to open from outside. A cocoon in which a person could while away the years, metabolism slowed, exterior time accelerated. A time machine in which to travel to the future.

For whom?

Nisbet wouldn't divulge the information and Carina didn't know. There was no reason for her to have been interested, but the decorations the box had carried made it important to Dumarest. As was the one now being completed. Later he would investigate.

It was after midnight when he rose and quietly slipped on his boots. The tavern was as silent as the town, which had died after the sounding of the curfew. Within moments the streets had been deserted. Now, lying behind closed shutters, the inhabitants waited until the dawn.

A board creaked as he left the room and he paused, listening. He heard nothing and moved on to halt at Carina's door. Beyond the panel he heard the soft, regular breathing of a person asleep and moved on to where stairs ran down into shrouded darkness.

Above there had been ghost-light from the stars filtering through cracks to create a pale, nacreous glow but down in the lower rooms of the tavern even that illumination was missing. Dumarest eased himself forward, hands extended, ears strained to catch the whisper of echoes. Like a blind man he moved toward the remembered door, found it, felt at the bolt which held it fast. It slipped back beneath his hand, the door gaping, closing again behind him as he passed outside.

The night was blazing with stars.

They covered the firmament with a golden glitter, gilded by the drifting spores which hued the air. Sheets and curtains of luminescence marred by the ebon blotches of interstellar dust. The heart of the Zaragoza Cluster with its multitude of worlds. Planets which had offered safety of a kind but a safety which could turn into a trap for a man without money. For a moment Dumarest looked at the burning stars, then moved away. What he searched for was not to be found in the cluster.

The street behind Nisbet's shop was as deserted as the rest of the town and Dumarest climbed the wall, dropping on the far side to wait, crouching, as he searched the area. Nothing. The windows shone with the dull gleam of reflected starlight and that was all. Rising, he moved to the big door facing the yard, tested it, moved on, when it remained fast, to the windows which ran beside it, found one that yielded beneath his hand.

A moment later he was inside a room which smelt of resin and spirit and gum and sawdust.

This was a storeroom with shelves supporting rows of bottles, cans, flasks of various sizes. Bins held rags and others tufted cotton. Drawers contained sheets of fine paper coated with dustlike abrasives. One corner smelt of assorted oils.

The door next to it opened beneath his hand and Dumarest moved softly through a thicker darkness to another which

opened on a room holding different smells. A third and he
was among inks and papers and the paraphernalia of an office. The desk was unlocked. By the starlight streaming
through the window he looked at papers taken from its
drawers.

They were in no sort of obvious order, and he frowned as
he tried to determine the reference system used. From the
look of things they had been stuffed at random into their
compartments: lists of material purchased, credits extended to
various workers, sums received and balances struck—normal
accounting to be found on any world using money as a
means of exchange.

He delved on, finding some elaborate designs traced on
thick parchments in faded inks: geometric patterns which had
little to commend them aside from their complexity. Others
were of living creatures, together with finely detailed depictions of joints and corner-pieces, dadoes, architraves, mitres
and other examples of the woodworker's art. As he reached
for another drawer he heard the soft scuffle of someone coming over the wall.

Dumarest froze, staring through the window, seeing in the
golden starlight an indistinct shape which ran lightly across
the yard in a direct path to the window by which he had entered. An apprentice, he guessed, and the reason for the un-
fastened window was plain. The youth had broken curfew,
leaving by the window he had left ajar for easy readmittance.
At the door of the office Dumarest rested his ear against the
panel, listening to the soft pad of feet, the rasp of the inner
door, the dying sounds of footsteps mounting the stairs.

Back at the desk he continued his search. The final drawer
yielded nothing of value and he stood, searching the office
with his eyes, trying to put himself in Nisbet's place. Work in
hand would mean the relevant papers would be within easy
reach. The desk was the obvious place but would a crafts-
man, impatient with office routine, follow the normal pattern?
The filing system he used was unique to himself and relied
wholly on memory. He had wasted time following accepted
patterns.

Where then?

Dumarest stepped from the office and into the area outside
where the air was heavy with the scent of wood and lacquer.
The box rested beneath a high row of narrow panes, starlight

touching a shelf, the folder lying on it. The first page held a printed slip, the second a list of specifications, the next was covered with designs, shapes which formed familiar symbols.

The Ram, the Bull, the Heavenly Twins and next the Crab the Lion shines, the Virgin and the Scales. The Scorpion, Archer and Sea Goat, the Man that holds the Watering Pot, the Fish with shining scales.

A mnemonic learned on a distant world. Symbols which represented the constellations as seen from Earth. One had led him to the Original People. He had seen them all when finding the spectrum of a forgotten sun.

These signs of the zodiac had decorated the box Carina had depicted.

Whoever had ordered them must know of Earth.

Chapter Six

Carina had been wrong; the ships began to arrive in days, not weeks, but the passengers they carried were not interested in the Sporing. They were the forefront of the flood to come, getting in early so as to complete their business. Shrewd-eyed men interested in local crafts hired rafts to carry them to outlying communes where they would live as guests, checking the times available, buying, trading, striking mutually satisfying bargains—dealers and entrepreneurs of all kinds. To control them and the crowds yet to come the Fathers of Caval had hired professional guards who now patrolled the streets, keeping the peace with words when possible, force when not.

"Serpents in a fair garden, Earl." Nubar Kusche, plump, bland, with graying hair roached and set with painstaking care over eyes which moved like liquid metal in time-stained sockets, shook his head as he stared down into the street from the balcony. "Vipers which betray the illusion of a Utopia. A pity that gentle consideration is too delicate a bloom to survive without protection."

Dumarest made no comment, staring as had Kusche at the street below, the environs beyond. The field was now busy and to one side the striped awnings of booths sprouted like a thrusting mass of exotic fungi. A carnival was to be expected on any world at such a time: a home for the gamblers and touts, the entertainers and artists who would harvest the fruits of the occasion. A lure for the local youth and a temptation the elders could have done without.

"Life," mused Kusche. "It goes on and who would stop it? But you are not drinking, my friend. Come, now, let me fill your glass!"

The act was done even as he spoke, the glint of his eyes matching the gleam of his teeth as he smiled. Kusche radiated an easy bonhomie and had shared a table with Dumarest the previous evening. He seemed to know all about Caval.

"Look at them!" He gestured toward a raft which lifted from the edge of the field and headed south. "Agents of the Romesh Syndicate, without a doubt. Heading into the Muuain and the Elton Hamlets. They hope to buy beads carved with delectable miniatures and nose-stones fashioned in the likeness of tiny birds. A forlorn quest."

"Because someone has got in first?"

"No. The craftsmen of the area have suffered this past season from an affliction of the eyes. Nothing serious, a form of ophthalmia, but it precluded fine and delicate work."

"Introduced by a previous visitor who will now return with the appropriate cure?"

"And so earn gratitude and a foothold in a lucrative market." Nubar Kusche beamed his appreciation of Dumarest's quick grasp of the situation. "You betray a shrewd knowledge of human nature, my friend. An asset on any world. But let me answer your unspoken query—it was not I who introduced the ophthalmia."

"But you know who did?" Dumarest watched the bland, unchanging smile. "You have to know—or why be so certain those men are on a forlorn quest? Not that it matters. I'm not after miniatures."

"Single pieces, then? If so I could guide you to certain favorable locations. The Weldach Village, for example. A long journey but, armed with the right goods and information, you could make a handsome profit."

"And you a fat commission?"

Kusche shrugged. "Why not? Surely you would not begrudge it? What have you to lose?"

The expenses of the trip, the trade goods purchased, time, lost opportunities—Dumarest was no stranger to what Kusche proposed.

He said, bluntly, "You're wasting your time."

"Allow me to be the judge of that. You have great potential, my friend. I recognize it. What would you say if I offered to stake you? A partnership, Earl. You would be interested in that?"

"It depends on the terms," said Dumarest. "I'd be interested in nothing less than for you to meet all costs. You provide the finance, I'll provide the labor and we split any profit made." He added, "One more thing—you hand over the money and I'll do all the shopping."

Inflating the bills and retaining the discounts—a sure way to make a profit no matter what the outcome of the trip. Something Kusche recognized.

"You are a hard man, my friend. The wine?"

"A debt I shall remember."

"Very hard." Nubar Kusche sighed and dabbed at his face with a square of embroidered silk. "Something I sensed on our first meeting, but a man must try. And no harm has been done." He smiled as he replaced the silk in a pocket. "A matter of practice and it is early days as yet. There will be others more interested in what I have to offer. And you?"

Dumarest returned the smile, shaking his head.

"A pity. We would make a good team, I think. If anything should come up and I should bump into you again—well, time enough for that when it happens. In the meantime there is work to be done." Kusche rose from the table and stood for a moment looking down into the street at the gaudy booths of the fair. "To deal," he said. "To trade. To lie a little in anticipation of the truth. The oldest profession, some say, though others would have it otherwise." He looked at a pavilion garish with phallic symbols which left no doubt as to the entertainment to be obtained inside. "Good luck, Earl."

"And to you, Nubar."

A genuine wish; Dumarest had no reason not to like the man. He was honest in his fashion and could not be blamed for what he was. An entrepreneur who was not too successful at the moment. His clothing showed telltale traces of wear, the rings he wore carried imitation gems, and he displayed a lack of judgment when selecting Dumarest as a potential victim. A mistake he had quickly realized but he had played the game to the end. A man with a stubborn streak and a sense of humor.

As he left the table Carina Davaranch took his place.

"A new friend, Earl?"

She had left him the previous afternoon to go about her

business and wore the same crimson dress she had then. He remembered it from Shard. Now, looking at her, he noted the lines of strain at the corners of her eyes, the tension of the muscles at lips and jaw. A tension which matched the tone of her voice.

"A chance acquaintance," he said. "Some wine?"

Kusche had left the bottle and a clean glass stood on a nearby table. Dumarest filled it and handed it to the woman.

As she took it she said bitterly, "Why are men such bastards?"

"Trouble?"

"The usual. They will buy my work—if. If I am complaisant. If I agree to doubling their commission. If I'm willing to wait." She drank half the wine. "This place is a jungle."

As were all worlds. Dumarest leaned back in his chair as he looked at her. Against the windows facing the balcony her reflection shone brightly gold and scarlet, the subtle touch of masculinity in her face and figure giving her an added depth of enigmatic attraction. Such a woman would be a challenge to every dealer she met—should they treat her as a normal female or regard her with the wary suspicion of a male?

She said, "I've had enough of this place, Earl. When you ship out I want to come with you. I guess you'll be moving soon. Right?"

There was no point in staying. Nisbet had known nothing more about the box than what Dumarest had learned and he'd gained more than the man was willing to tell. The folder had yielded only specifications, the printed sheet listing dates and the name of the agency handling the transaction. The Huag-Chi-Tsacowa—they had an office in town. From it Dumarest had learned that all cost-data were held in the computer of the depot on Brundel. Only they would know the name and whereabouts of the owner of the casket.

Details he didn't mention. Instead, he said, "Why don't you stay here, Carina?"

"I told you. I've had enough of this place. And we've been through that before. I'm a free agent and when I want to move then I damned well move." She drank the rest of her wine. "I can book passage on any vessel I choose."

"If they're willing to take you."

"I've money enough to make sure of that." She smiled,

confident, then lost the smile as she saw his expression. "Earl?"

"I've made my plans, Carina."

"And they don't include me, is that it?" She blinked and swallowed to master her hurt. "Am I asking so much? All I want is to ride with you. To have some decent company on the journey. I guess you could say I need a friend. Is that so hard to understand?"

One journey leading to another, to more, the friend becoming a responsibility, a burden that he had no intention of bearing.

He said, bluntly, "It ends here. Our association, I mean. I go my way and you go yours." He rose and stood looking down at her. "That's the way travelers are."

"Yes." She took a deep breath then, smiling, rose to stand at his side. Chairs hampered movement and she stepped from the table to the open space before the line of windows. "You're right, Earl. I'm sorry—it's just that I've had too many hassles these past few hours. Well, let's forget it. But there's one thing I'd like to do before we part."

"What?"

She smiled again in answer and took his hand and led him to a space before a window. People moved around, some men, a bunch of women, youngsters staring at the displayed goods with sparkling eyes. Staring too at the dim shapes moving behind the darkened pane which held mirror-like reflections.

Carina ignored them as she moved to stand between the window and Dumarest. In the pane he could see the sheen of her golden hair, the naked expanse of flesh between it and the top of her gown, the small bones of her spine, the hollow at the nape of her neck. Muscles shifted beneath her skin as she raised her hands to rest on his shoulders.

"Kiss me, Earl. Before we part—kiss me!"

For the first and last time. The golden helmet of her hair tilted as she turned her face upwards toward him. Her lips, pursed, were inches from his own.

In the window something moved.

The reflection of a man who stepped forward with sudden determination, his right hand lifted, metallic gleams coming from what he held.

Dumarest saw him, recognized the danger and acted with

instinctive speed, his reaction free of the hampering need of thought. As the glittering object neared the back of his neck he spun, the woman in his arms, the charge of the hypogun driving through her skin and fat into her blood as the man pressed the trigger. A shield Dumarest threw to one side as she slumped in his arms.

Before the man could fire again he was within reach. Dumarest slammed up his left hand, catching the wrist, sending the hypogun to rise in a spinning arc as his right hand rose, fingers and palm bent backwards to form a right angle, the heel smashing with stunning, bone-breaking force against the exposed jaw.

As the man fell a woman screamed.

She stood to one side, a plump matron neatly dressed, hands and throat bright with precious metals and sparkling gems. A woman with a high regard for beauty, now ugly as she stood and shrieked and pointed at Dumarest with a shaking hand.

"Murderer! He killed them both! Guards! Where are the guards?"

A false accusation that Dumarest had no time to correct. A man joined the woman in sounding the alarm and another, more courageous than wise, ran forward with one hand lifted, the other snatching at a weapon carried beneath his tunic.

A laser he had no time to use—it fell to one side as Dumarest struck, hitting to stun and not to kill. Two other men changed their minds as the man fell and joined in the general summons for guards. From below came the sharp blast of a whistle, another from the far end of the balcony.

Dumarest ran forward and saw the uniformed shape, spotted another in the street below. Soon there would be more; men accustomed to violence, ready to stun and maim to keep the peace. To kill if the need arose. He turned as more whistles echoed from the distance, running to the rail edging the balcony, judging time and distance and springing over the barrier to land with a bone-jarring impact on the street below. Rising, he staggered two steps and then was running, dodging between startled pedestrians, thrusting his way into an alley, emerging to find an open-fronted emporium, to slow and halt as he inspected a hanging mass of loose garments.

"You are interested, sir?" The owner, scenting a sale, bustled forward. "For your wife, perhaps? Your daughter?"

"My wife." Dumarest shook his head. "She's a large woman and these seem to be too small."

"I have larger in the rear." The man frowned at the sound of whistles, the thud of running boots. "Such noise! Such confusion! Well, it will soon be over. After you, sir?"

Dumarest reached the rear of the shop as a guard halted in the street outside. The man knew his job and did more than just stare. The owner shrilled his anger as the man prodded the hanging garments with his club. It was a loaded length of wood, inches thick and a yard long, a weapon which could shatter bone and smash a skull.

"Be careful! Those are garments of price! What are you looking for?" He gestured in response to the answer. "He's not here. Be off now! Off!"

Dumarest said, as the man came toward him, "I'll take this one. And this." He pointed at the selected garments. The price?"

It was too high but he didn't argue, knowing he paid for more than cloth. "And this." He took a loose robe which covered him from neck to toe with a hood to shield his head. A garment to disguise his betraying gray. "I'll take this with me and send for the other things later. How much in all?"

The emporium had a back door and the owner guided Dumarest through it. A bonus to compensate for the fact the two female robes would never be collected. The street beyond was narrow and winding, flanked with enigmatic doors and opaque windows. A bad place in which to be trapped, and Dumarest was relieved when he reached a junction and saw the silhouettes of ships against the sky. Beyond them lay the gaudy awnings of the carnival booths and, among them, he would find a degree of safety.

"This way, handsome." The voice of the crone was a mechanical drone over the rising blasts of whistles. "Come and let old Mother Kekrop read your fortune. Life and luck, and pleasant surprises. Learn of the dangers at hand. Share in—"

Dumarest said, "I know of the dangers at hand. I can hear them. What chance of a snug crib?"

She stared, blinking, at Dumarest's face wreathed in the

hood. It was not what she'd expected. "Those whistles for you?"

"I worked a con and the mark got peeved. I need to hide out for a while." Dumarest added, "I can pay."

"You carny?"

"I've run a booth and drawn an edge. Grafted with the best and handled my share of punters." His talk and slang won her confidence. "I need a hand, Mother."

As the whistles drew near she said, "In the back. You'll find a slit, go through it, ask for Zather in the next booth. Move!"

Her drone rose again as Dumarest followed instructions. "This way, young man. Let old Mother Kekrop read your fortune. The secret of the future lies in the palm of your hand." The drone turned shrill. "Bastard! Mind where you put that club!"

Zather was old and shrewd with a drooping eyelid and gemmed rings in his ears. He looked once at Dumarest then said. "Fifty will buy you safety until the heat's off. Got it?" He grunted as Dumarest handed over the money. "No argument?"

"Not unless you cheat me."

"Then what?"

"I'll resent it." A chair stood to one side and Dumarest lifted his right boot and set it on the seat. The hilt of his knife was plainly visible.

"A knife-man." Zather looked at the weapon. "A fighter, maybe?"

"I've worked a ring."

"Good." Zather lifted his voice. "Lucita! Bring in the board and some knives!" To Dumarest he said, "I'd like to see what you can do."

The girl came from an adjoining booth carrying a board of soft wood half as high again as a man and proportionately wide. She was young, well-shaped, with dark, smoldering eyes and long glistening hair which hung in an ebon cascade over rounded shoulders. With the board she had carried a half-dozen knives which she handed to Dumarest.

Taking them he said, "Mark the board. Six points you want me to hit."

While she was busy he examined the knives. They were well-made finely balanced tools designed for a specific purpose. As the girl straightened and moved aside Dumarest threw each one directly into its target.

"Neat." Zather was impressed. "How are you in combat? Can you stretch a bout, take a wound, fake a decision? If you're good I could use you. A place in the booth on equal terms with the rest. No questions and good eating. Think about it." He jerked his head at the girl as drums pounded from somewhere near at hand. "Get ready, girl! You're about due to go on." To Dumarest he said, "Wait here. I'll send someone to move you to a safer place."

"Not to the bordello."

"You object?"

"Not on moral grounds but it'll be the first place the guards will search."

"Smart." Zather nodded his approval. "You've got brains. A fool wouldn't have thought of that. Well, don't worry, you'll be taken good care of."

A boy came later to guide Dumarest to another booth, weaving through a succession of tents and narrow passages and once across open ground after making certain it was clear. Huddled in his robe Dumarest followed, sensing the growing activity of the carnival. The familiar atmosphere spelled security. In another place fitted with a bed and tables, chairs and portable washing facilities, the boy left to return with a bowl of stew and a hunk of crusty bread together with a bottle of good red wine.

Lucita joined him as he finished the stew. She wore bright and flimsy clothing which she removed to stand naked in casual abandon.

"Do you mind?"

"No." Dumarest looked at the furnishings which betrayed a feminine touch. "Your place?"

"And yours until it's time for you to move." Water gushed into the bowl as she manipulated the taps. "I hate to sweat; it makes me feel all sticky. Can you take care of my back?" She arched it as he ran the sponge over the smooth skin. "That's nice. I wish I had you around all the time. You going to stay?"

"I might."

"I'd like it if you did. We could work together. Do really well at it. You in the ring acting up and fixing the bouts and

me on the outside with the punters. I'd grab a prime mark
and distract him and get him to plunge on the wrong man.
You think I could?"

Dumarest looked at the face she turned toward him, the
deep cleavage of her breasts, the swell of her hips. Of more
moment was the expression in her eyes, the warmly promis-
ing and excitingly wanton look of a world-wise and experienced woman.

"Yes," he said, smiling. "You most certainly could."

"I like you," she said. "If you like me we can make music.
Later, when you've decided to stay. Zather couldn't object
then."

"He your father?"

"My owner. He bought me when I was just a kid." Her
breasts lifted as she raised her hands to tidy her hair. "You
could buy me off him once we make our pile. I'd be good to
you. What I need is a man hard enough to be respected but
gentle at the right times. One jealous enough to be flattering
but not so jealous as to be stupid. You know what I mean?
You've got to milk the edge at times. Take the pitch for all
you can get. Jealousy at the wrong time would spoil that."
She frowned as a trumpet blared from outside. "Damn! I'm
on again. Be good, handsome—and be here when I get
back!"

She flounced out dressed in spangles and glitter and garish
paint. Alone, Dumarest opened the wine and sipped, waiting
until it had reached his stomach before taking a swallow. The
bed was soft but he chose to use the floor, sitting with his
back against a pole, legs extended, the bottle standing to one
side within reach of his hand. There was nothing he could do.
To rise and move around would be to negate the security he
had paid for.

He slept, resting like an animal, hovering on the brink of
wakefulness until the sounds from outside became a part of
his universe. Disrupted, they screamed a warning which sent
Dumarest to his feet.

"The bastards!" A woman was crying beyond the wall of
fabric. "The dirty bastards! They didn't have to do that!"

Another sound, the deep, menacing rumble of a carnival
alerted to danger. From somewhere a man cursed and glass
made a brittle music as it crashed to ruin. A booth ruined in

some kind of struggle. Guards on the rampage, perhaps, but why?

Dumarest tensed as a figure came into the room, relaxed a little as he recognized Zather.

"Trouble?"

"Nothing we can't handle. Some drunks acting up and a party from one of the ships trying out their muscle." Zather sucked in his breath as shouting flared, to die and rise again farther away. "The boys will take care of it and collect what's due. That isn't why I' here." He paused, then said, "You'll have to move. I can't hide you."

The girl? Was Zather concerned?

Dumarest said, "What's gone wrong?"

"You lied. I don't know who you killed out there but it was no peeved mark. I figured the guards would give up after a while and things would die down. They haven't. There's a reward out for you and it's too big to be ignored. A cool thousand. I couldn't even trust myself with that kind of money at stake. Someone will get greedy and if they pass the word you've had it. And so have we if you should be found. Sorry, but there it is."

"You want me to go?"

"That's what I'm saying. It's dark now and I can guide you to the edge of the field. After that you're on your own." Zather hesitated, then added. "Just one thing. Those guards are Scafellians. Mean bastards every last one of them. Hurt one and the rest will beat you to a jelly. Leave you crippled for life, blind, deaf—they like to maintain their reputation. I just thought I'd warn you."

"Thanks," said Dumarest. "Now give me back my money."

Chapter Seven

———— ·•◆•· ————

Rain had come with the darkness, a drizzle which haloed the lights with miniature rainbows and caused the pennons to hang limp from their poles. The dampness did little to hurt the carnival; the sounds seemed to hang louder because of it. Shouts, laughter, screams caused by excitement as well as by anger and pain. Men and women enjoying a time of fantasy in which each was a winner and all prizes made of diamond and gold.

A normal scene aside from the guards.

They were everywhere, restless, patrolling with quick impatience as if afraid some other of their number would capture the prize. A thousand cren—more than double what they could earn in a year. Who wanted him enough to put up such a reward?

Dumarest waited, crossed an open space, stooped, huddled in his robe, one foot dragging as if lame. Slight deceptions but they would help if a guard was concentrating too hard on finding someone of a certain height, a certain build. Shadows closed around him and he paused to check the area. Before him lay the field, the ships resting on the dirt. Unlike more civilized worlds there was no perimeter fence; but this bonus was offset by the number of guards moving between the vessels and the size of the posted reward.

To his left, closer to the town, warehouses squatted like eyeless beasts and Dumarest stared at them with thoughtful attention. If empty they could be open and maybe patrolled but the interiors would provide nooks and crannies in which

68

to hide. Something the guards would know and so be on the alert. But, if full?

A possibility and later he would consider it but, for now, there were more urgent problems.

Dumarest moved, heading for an avenue leading to town, as the sound of boots together with flashing lights became recognizable to his right. The avenue was wide, set with benches and flowering shrubs, a favorite spot for young lovers to stroll in balmy evenings. Now they were enjoying the carnival but the benches remained as did the shrubs. Dumarest reached a cluster and crouched down among them. It was as good a place as any to spend the night.

Time dragged. At midnight the rain eased and finally ceased, the sky clearing to permit the faint glow of stars. In the soft light he was just a shadow among shadows and three times patrolling guards passed within a few feet of where he crouched. Once, a light shone on his body but the man behind it saw only the shrubs he knew were there.

That moment of tension passed as the guards moved on and Dumarest had time to renew his thoughts.

Had Carina deliberately betrayed him?

The kiss could have been a signal to the man with the hypogun but why had she delayed so long? Was it because he had ended their association? Or had the man only just arrived, following the girl so as to find his quarry, striking when he had?

To have attacked the man could have been a mistake; Dumarest could have dodged and found some other way to avoid the numbing drug he was certain the hypogun had carried. Yet it would have made little difference—once the trap had been sprung he'd had no choice but to react.

Leaning back, he looked at the sky, now dotted with pale and golden points of brilliance. Beyond them, as if in a nightmare, he saw another universe, one covered by a scarlet web, strands reaching from world to world and, at the nexus, a scarlet shape—robed and cowled but without a face. A figure of brooding menace from which extensions multiplied its presence and spawned a scarlet tide. A thing from which he had run to become enmeshed, to break free and run again and again to find himself in a trap.

Had the Cyclan known he was on Shard?

There had been no cybers on the planet, few in the Zaragoza Cluster; poor worlds held little attraction to an organization dedicated to the pursuit of power. But each time he moved he left a trail and from it any cyber could extrapolate the logical sequence of his future actions. Ships followed known routes, agents would report, data could be assimilated and assessed—had they lured him to Caval?

Using a bait he was unable to resist?

Even knowing the world was a trap, he would have been driven to take a chance. To know. To *know*—nothing else mattered. To find the answer for which he searched. The owner of the box could have it.

The coordinates of Earth.

Knowing him, the Cyclan must know of his quest and could have used that information to lure him to a world of its choice. But would they have fashioned the boxes? Set Nisbet to wait until he arrived and then to be so unhelpful? Arranged the details of an entire living complex on the assumption that he would learn of the casket and the decoration it had carried?

He decided not. The box he'd examined had been real and there had been more than one. And while the Cyclan held greater power than any other organization ever known, it was not omnipotent.

No matter how the trap had been arranged there was now only one matter of real importance—how to escape.

The bird chirrupped, tilted its head, stared with a beady eye at the shape below which remained so still. A sound which joined with others to break the pre-dawn stillness. Dumarest took advantage of it to ease his weight and change his stance. Small movements which pressed his boots against the gravel to produce a faint rasping, echoed by the sound of boots from lower down the warehouse.

Guards and Dumarest tensed. So far he'd been lucky, moving when no one could see, freezing to stand immobile in the shadows the searchers passed by. Too many and still too intent. A second shift, he guessed, fresh men to replace those tired and jaded. Fatigue he had assessed when moving from the shrubs to the avenue. Now, among the warehouses, his skin prickled to incipient danger.

"A waste of time." The voice echoed disgust. "I bet he's

holed up in that carnival. Instead of checking the town and field we should go in and take the damned place apart."

"Give them the fun of the fair, eh, Franz?"

"Why not? You like the idea of them laughing at us?"

"They won't be laughing for long." The second voice held a feral purr. "But the grounds and booths were checked last night and nothing found."

"So?"

"So we wait until dawn and then go in. A full cordon and the orders are not to be gentle. If he was there someone will tell us. If we find him the place gets burned." The man laughed with a soft malice. "My bet is that it gets burned in any case. An accident—you know how they can happen."

Franz returned the laughter. "Too well, Tousel. It should be fun."

Two of them and there could be more within call. The Scafellians were efficient. Dumarest listened to the pad of nearing boots and saw the flash of beams directed at the looming bulk of the warehouse against which he stood. Lights which rose to the eaves as well as playing on the lower regions.

Deep in the shadows something snarled and broke free with a rasp of claws. A nocturnal predator startled by the noise and confused by the lights. It raced across the gravel toward the place where Dumarest stood, slowed as it scented his presence and sprang upward to hit the wall with all four feet. As it vanished over the eaves the darting beams followed it, one sliding down to follow the trail left in the scuffed gravel. Before it could reach him Dumarest stepped forward.

"You there! Halt!" The rasp in his tone was that of one accustomed to obedience. "Lower those beams! Immediately!"

Automatically they obeyed.

"Your numbers?" Dumarest waited as they gave them. "I am reporting you both for gross negligence. Do you think the man we are searching for is deaf? I heard your babble long before you appeared. Had I been the criminal I could have killed you both. Fools! Return to your checkpoint and report to your officer."

It almost worked. If he had worn a familiar uniform they would have obeyed but the robe was soiled and creased and Franz had seen too much in the diffused glow of his torch.

"Your authority, sir? Your name?"

"Major Wyle—I am known."

Franz hesitated. The man had stepped forward without being challenged and it was not uncommon for spot checks to be made. And they had been talking too loudly. Yet he was reluctant to compound the error.

Tousel solved the dilemma. "Your identification, sir? Please show me your identification."

"Of course." Dumarest stepped closer to the guards as he fumbled beneath the robe. One, the elder, stood back, both hands on his club, which he carried like a stave before him. The standard alert-stance from which he could move in any direction and bring his weapon into play with maximum efficiency. The other had taken a step forward, one hand extended, the club dangling from its thong. "I wondered when you would ask for it. Your light?"

Dumarest moved on as Tousel aimed his torch to illuminate his robe. The elder of the two hadn't moved but his eyes shifted a little as Dumarest drew closer. The more wary of the two, he must be taken care of first.

"Here," said Dumarest. "Check this."

His hand came from beneath the robe, fingers clenched as if holding something, his arm extending as he neared the watchful guard. Another step and the fingers had straightened to form a blunted spear which he thrust up and forward to strike at the throat, at the nerves buried deep beneath the skin. He delivered the blow with lightning speed and the man was falling before Tousel knew what was happening. Even so he was fast.

"Alarm!" he shouted. "To me! Al—"

He slumped, stunned, not feeling the impact of the gravel, but the damage had been done. From the far end of the warehouse came the dancing glow of lights, accompanied by the blare of whistles. Dumarest glanced the other way, saw more lights signalling more guards. Trapped between them, he had only one way left to go.

He backed, breathing deeply, knowing he would have only this one chance. Before him the building loomed dark against the sky and it was hard to spot the exact position of the eaves. A run and he threw himself upwards, hands extended, feeling the bruising impact of the wall against legs and chest as the tips of his fingers caught the gutter. For a moment he hung suspended, then, with a convulsive effort, had drawn himself up and over the eaves to lie sprawled on the low slope of the roof.

Above him something snarled.

The creature which had betrayed him, startled then and furious now. Dumarest heard the rasp of claws and swung up a hand, striking fur, hearing the beast land and dart away.

"What was that?" A guard below swung up the beam of his light. "I heard something up there. It—" The beam jerked as the creature jumped from the roof, chasing it as it landed to race into darkness. "There! He's running down there!"

A natural mistake, and Dumarest lay silent as the guards ran after the vanished beast.

Dawn came to illuminate the warehouse, one of a row set widely apart, the spaces between patrolled by guards. Dumarest watched them, careful not to reveal himself against the sky, checking the distance between himself and the field with its ships. Safety lay there if he could reach them and find a handler willing to give him passage. One wise enough to know that he would never get the posted reward for handing over the wanted man. To insist would be to wait for the hearing, wait for the final assessment and then with luck, to receive only a portion. Professional guards did not take kindly to those wanting to deprive them of their rewards.

The problem lay in choosing the right vessel. That was the first problem—there were others: to reach it unseen, to gain time to make the arrangements, to stay free until it left. But first, to find the right ship.

Dumarest studied them from his position on the roof: a freighter which would carry massed cargoes, some free traders open to charter, an agency vessel belonging to a trading consortium, a couple of others he guessed had been hired for a specific task. The dealers who had come to trade and buy would not wait for the Sporing but once they had gone it would be a long time before the tourists followed. If he was to escape it had to be soon.

Dumarest looked at the sky, at the wheeling shapes of birds and other shapes which rose to glide low and steady through the air. Rafts filled with watching men who would search every inch of open ground.

The roof was thin; corrugated metal heavily painted to provide protection against the elements. Inset panels of transparent glass provided light for the interior of the building. Dumarest reached one, tested the edge and found it bolted firm. Given time he could have found one not so fast but he had no time. Stripping off the hampering robe, he bundled it around his fist, punched, felt glass yield beneath the blow. Carefully he widened the opening and, using the robe to protect his hands, swung himself down through the shattered pane. A short drop and he landed in a shadowed dimness filled with crates and bales and enigmatic packages—goods waiting shipment. Soon the building would be bright with light from the rising sun. Dumarest moved among the stacks looking for something light enough to carry yet large enough to provide cover. A burden suitable for one man and an excuse for him to cross the field and reach the ships. A weak excuse but if he could find clothes to fit the part and others he could join, it offered a chance.

He tensed as something hammered on the door, the sound yielding to the rumble of voices.

"Quit that, Palmer! You want to warn him?"

"If he's in there." The voice held disgust. "How the hell could he be?"

"The same way he got free of Franz and Tousel. With brains and guts, that's how. Two experienced men like that and they let him get away. Do the same and you'll join them in punishment."

"But a sealed building?"

"Just obey orders. Once the area has been checked from the air we search each warehouse in turn. In the meantime no one is to enter or leave under any pretext. Got that? No loading—the damn ships can wait."

A trap and Dumarest was in it. He glanced at the broken skylight—once spotted from the air they would have him located and the rest would be only a matter of time. How to get clear? A guard? Called in, knocked out, his uniform taken—but no, guards operated in pairs and now they would be extra cautious. Use gas before entering the building, perhaps—vapors to induce sleep and knock out anyone inside.

Again Dumarest examined the building, looking for something, anything, to use in the emergency. A heap of bales stood to one side and he squeezed behind them, following a narrow passage to a cleared space littered with bindings, ropes and padding. Resting amid the litter stood the unmistakable shape of a familiar casket.

The one Carina had painted.

It had to be that—the decorations were complete, and he moved around it, checking, thinking. Finished, it had been shifted to the warehouse from the Hurich Complex to wait shipment from Caval. The Huag-Chi-Tsacowa was an efficient company and would not have wanted to cause their client the high expense of a special charter. What did a few weeks matter? The casket could wait until the traders arrived and be added to other cargo for shipment.

A logical explanation—ships would have been few before the Sporing and none would have urgent reason to go where the casket was bound. Brundel? No, that was the depot but not necessarily the casket's final destination. Where then? Where?

Dumarest searched the exterior of the box, scanning the decorations, the carvings, the smoothly finished surfaces for some clue as to its final destination. He saw nothing but the sticker bearing the Huag-Chi-Tsacowa sigil. Later the casket would be wrapped in protective padding, and he probed the litter, finding nothing of help. As he straightened, he heard the dull clang of shifting metal from the doors.

"Steady now!" The voice held a brisk efficiency. "If you spot him stand well clear. There's no sense in getting hurt. We'll bring him down with gas and nets and split the reward. Any fool who acts the hero will deserve all he gets."

Another guard said, "He won't try anything once he knows he's cornered."

"Believe that and you could wind up dead. Spread out and watch the roof. He could be clinging to a strut. Check each pile of bales and make sure he isn't on the top. Watch to see he doesn't leap from one to another. If he's in here we'll all be sharing a nice bonus."

A prediction—the guards would make no mistakes. Dumarest glanced at the roof, the skylights now bright with sunlight. Even if he could reach one unseen and make his way outside he would be spotted from the air. To try to reach the door would be to invite capture. To fight was to be maimed.

Dumarest stepped toward the casket, remembering the

details he had gained from the folder. Luck was with him, the lid rose with silent ease to reveal the interior, padded and bright with a nacreous sheen. A moment and he was inside, the lid closing as the guards came near.

Chapter Eight

Like a swimmer rising from the floor of an incredible sea, Dumarest floated upward through layers of ebon chill, waiting for the warming impact of eddy currents, praying the handler had administered the numbing drugs which alone could prevent the searing agony of returning circulation. The journey would end either in the burning euphoria of resurrection or the oblivion of death.

A nightmare which yielded to a soft and reassuring comfort. The layers of ebon chill turned into bands and swathes of rainbow color, a kaleidoscope filled with unexpected delights and enticing novelties. The handler became a benign figure who smiled and extended a hand and radiated a warm bonhomie—with a familiar face.

"It's time, Earl," said Nubar Kusche. "Time for you to wake up."

To wake and stretch and to remember a plethora of dreams. Of faces which had come to him in scented darkness and scenes fashioned in a world of kindly benevolence. Of a man who had helped and guided his stumbling footsteps and a woman who had tended him with the loving care of an angel. Snatches of a childhood he had never experienced, of a father he had never known, of a mother who had died too soon. Dreams to comfort and entertain as there had been others: adventures in which he had strode through gilded courts in heroic guise to be adored by nubile women and admired by noted warriors.

And Kalin had come to him. Kalin with the flame-red hair

77

and the deep, sea-green eyes. The woman he had loved and who, loving him, had bequeathed him the secret which had made him the most hunted man in the galaxy.

"Earl?" Kusche looked anxious. "Earl—you know me?"

Dumarest looked at the face, the tracery of minute lines, the eyes set beneath their prominent brows, the shape of the lips, the chin, the line of the jaw, small details he had ignored before but which could now mean his life.

"No!" Kusche, watching in turn, had recognized the warning of the eyes, the cruel set of the mouth. "No, Earl, you have nothing to fear from me. I am your friend. I swear it."

Words, a part of any entrepreneur's stock in trade, as was the easy smile, the radiated assurance. Dumarest looked beyond the face which hung suspended over the open casket, haloed with a soft effulgence which turned the gray mass of his roached hair into a crest of tarnished silver. Behind reared a featureless wall of dull olive, a ceiling of glowing azure. The air, while crisp, did not strike chill and held the scent of roses and pine.

"Where is this?"

"A place, Earl." Kusche beamed his relief as he answered the question. "A safe place."

"How long?"

"Long enough for you to have left Caval. Can you rise? Sit up? Come, this is no place to talk. We need wine and delicacies and soft furnishings to celebrate the moment. Come!" He stepped back as Dumarest knocked aside his hand and stood watching as the other left the casket. "This way, my friend."

He led Dumarest to a passage opening on a room containing a bath, in which Dumarest soaked. The room was fitted with a table and chairs and drifting light from a revolving fabrication which painted the furnishings with bright and changing hues.

"You must be full of questions," said Kusche as he poured wine. "And I am here to answer them. First, my congratulations for having escaped the guards on Caval. A demonstration of your ability to survive which can only be admired. To have assessed the situation, to have acted with such promptness, to have utilized all available means of help and to have recognized the one remaining way of eluding capture—a worthy achievement. Here." He handed Dumarest a goblet. "I drink to you, my friend. To you and to the happy accident which drew us together."

A toast Dumarest ignored. As Kusche lowered his goblet he said, "Where are we?"

"On Zabul."

"And you?"

"I am here as your friend, Earl. As your attendant. As your guide." Then, as Dumarest made no comment, Kusche added, "At times we manipulate fate and, at others, we are directed in turn. A matter of coincidence and fortuitous circumstances. If we hadn't met and shared wine on that balcony. If I hadn't been what I am and guessed certain things and, yes, taken my opportunity when I recognized it, I wouldn't be here facing you now. Fate, my friend; at times it governs us all."

The wine was amber flecked with motes of emerald. Dumarest touched it to his lips and tasted a sweet astringency.

"You say nothing," mused Kusche. "In that you are wise. How often has a man sold himself short by his inability to remain silent? Jumped to the wrong conclusion by his reluctance to wait? First let us dispose of the casket. You must know or have guessed how they operate. When you closed the lid you locked yourself in a sealed environment which could only be broken by the lapse of time, conscious effort or skilled intervention." He drank a mouthful of his wine. "When the guards searched the warehouse they found nothing but a sealed box which they could not open. Obviously, therefore, you could not have been inside it. Naturally they concluded the broken skylight was a decoy and you had moved on to hide elsewhere."

"And?"

Kusche shrugged. "The traders began to leave and the assembled cargo with them. The Huag-Chi-Tsacowa shipped the casket from Caval. You see, my friend, it is all so very simple."

All but for the one fact he had carefully not mentioned. Dumarest said bluntly, "And you? How did you know I was in the box?"

After a moment of hesitation Kusche said blandly, "A matter of logic, Earl. Where else could you have been?"

Logic which the entrepreneur might have the ability to exercise but in Dumarest's experience, only one type of man could have been so certain of the strength of his prediction.

Was Kusche a cyber?

A possibility Dumarest considered while toying with his wine. The man wore ordinary clothing but a scarlet robe could be removed and hair allowed to grow on a shaven scalp. Emotions, too, could be counterfeited and yet his instinct told him the man was what he seemed. No cyber would ape the type of person he despised. If not pride then respect for his organization would make him cling to his robe, the fellowship with others of his kind.

And if Kusche was a cyber, why the wine, the delicacies, the talk? If the casket had been delivered into the hands of the Cyclan there would be no need of this charade.

And yet—why was he here?

Kusche met his eyes as, bluntly, Dumarest asked the question. He was as blunt in his answer.

"For profit, Earl. For gain. It was obvious you are no ordinary criminal. The guards were too eager, the reward too high. If you are so valuable to those who wanted you captured it seemed advisable for me to become your partner. In helping you I would be helping myself." His tone grew bitter. "A simple plan—how was I to guess at the complications? All I wanted was to ride with you and be at hand when you left the casket. To talk about us making a deal. But the Huag-Chi-Tsacowa proved most uncooperative and it cost a fortune in bribes. Wasted money."

"But you got here."

"No, Earl, I was brought." Kusche looked at his hands, at the gemmed ring adorning the left one. "I don't remember much about it. I was asleep, then I woke up here in a room like this. A man questioned me and told me this was Zabul. Then I was taken to the casket and the rest you know." He added, "There's one more thing. The man I saw is coming to ask you a question. He asked it of me and I stalled and put the answer on you. One question, Earl—they're crazy!"

"Who are?"

"The people who live here. The man I saw. That question, Earl, he meant it. One damned question." Kusche reached for his wine and drank and sat staring into the empty goblet. He said dully, "He wanted me to give him one reason why I should be allowed to stay alive."

In the dreams there had been music: deep threnodies emulating the restless surge of mighty oceans, the wail of keening winds, the susurration of rippling grasses, the murmur of somnolent bees. Sounds captured by the sensory apparatus and translated to fit into the pattern of electronically stimulated fantasies. Now Dumarest heard it again as, rising, he paced the room.

It was small, a score of feet on a side, the roof less than half as high. A chamber decorated with the neat precision of one accustomed to regimented tidiness. One which could have belonged to a person of either sex but of a narrow field of profession.

Dumarest touched the wall with the tips of his fingers, frowned, knelt to examine the floor. Without looking at Nubar Kusche, he said, "Have you ever seen a window? Looked outside?"

"No."

"They just told you this was Zabul?"

"He told me, Earl. Urich Volodya. The one who asked that damned stupid question." He added, "He's the only one I've seen."

Rising, Dumarest walked to where the outline of a door marred the smooth perfection of a wall. It was locked. The bathroom was as he had left it but the door to the room holding the casket was closed and sealed. Back with Kusche he listened again to the music, which seemed to originate in the very air—a vibration carried by a trick of acoustics or a lingering hallucination from his recent dreams.

To Kusche he said, "How long has it been since you saw Volodya?"

"Not long. He took me to the casket to wait until it opened—that was about fifteen minutes. Then you had that bath and we talked."

"And before that?"

"When he asked me the question? About five hours."

"Was he serious?"

"Yes." Kusche was emphatic. "I know it sounds crazy but it's the truth. One question—and I couldn't think of a single answer!"

But he had talked his way out of the necessity of answering, or Volodya had spared him to cushion his own shock of waking. To be what he had claimed, a mentor, friend and guide. But why?

Dumarest shook his head, irritated by the music, the whispering chords with their associations. A danger he recognized, and he forced himself to relax. Uncontrolled anger could lead to fatal errors, and if Kusche was telling the truth he would need all his wits. But there was no reason to play the game according to an opponent's rules.

He said, "We're supposed to sit and wait and sweat. Well, to hell with them. Got a deck?" He took the cards Kusche produced. "What shall it be?"

"Man-in-between."

Dumarest dealt: a ten to his left, a four to his right, a lady between the two. "High wins." A lord to his left, a trey to his right, a seven last. "Man-in-between." A jester and two eights. "High wins." A pair of nines and a deuce. "Low wins."

An easy, monotonous, boring game. Before he had dealt the pack three times the door opened and Urich Volodya entered the room.

He was tall with a slender grace and a carriage dictated by position and breeding. A man with the long, flat muscles of a runner and the sharp features of a questing idol. The nose was thin, beaked, the eyes hooded beneath jutting brows. The chin was strong as was the mouth, the line of the jaw. A high forehead was made higher by a mane of fine dark hair which rested in neat curls on a peaked skull. His clothing was somber but rich. He radiated an almost tangible sense of power and authority.

Ignoring him, Dumarest turned over another card.

"Ace," he said. "High wins."

Kusche was uneasy. "Earl, we're not alone."

"I know that. You want to make your bet or answer a stupid question?" Dumarest finished the deal. "Low wins."

"Earl Dumarest," said Volodya. "So you think my question was stupid?"

"It is always stupid to threaten a man's life." Dumarest dropped the cards and rose to face the visitor. "He could take offense," he explained mildly. "He could even decide to do something about it."

"Such as getting in first?"

"It could happen."

"But not here and not to me. Surely it isn't necessary for me to point out that I am not unprotected? Lift a hand against me and those watching will burn it from your arm. Need I say more?"

A possible bluff but the man could be speaking the truth; his arrogance indicated he was. He seemed to have the conviction, too, that all men held life above all other considerations—a fault which had caused many rulers to run blindly to their destruction.

"Before we continue our discussion let me point out certain facts," continued Volodya. "For one, you are guilty of trespass in that you used a casket not your own without permission. For another, you are here without invitation. For a third, you are both an inconvenience. Zabul is a private place and we do not welcome visitors. Still less do we relish gossip and idle conversation which could lead to unwanted curiosity. However, we try to be just. We could have destroyed you without hesitation—instead we offer a chance for survival. Do you still consider the question to be stupid?"

Dumarest said, "You want me to give you one good reason why I should be allowed to stay alive. Is that it?"

"Why you should both be allowed to stay alive," corrected Volodya. "Your friend has abrogated his right of reply to you. A heavy burden, but a fair one. If a man cannot justify his existence then why should he demand the right to continue it?"

"Demand of whom? God?"

"Here, in this place, as Guardian of the Terridae, I have the power of life and death over all in the domain of Zabul. You would do well to believe that. To believe also in the seriousness of your situation." Volodya paused. "You have three minutes in which to think of your answer."

Three minutes in which to prepare for death and Dumarest knew it. The answer wanted was one not even a trained philosopher could supply. Volodya was playing a game to ease his conscience or to enhance his standing in his own eyes. To act the god. To cater to a sadistic trait even though he would be the first to deny it.

From behind him Kusche whispered, "Think of something, Earl. For God's sake—he means it!"

Dumarest sagged a little, his right hand lowering, fingers nearing the hilt of the knife carried in his boot. A forlorn defense but if he was to die then he would do his best to take Volodya with him. To kill the Proud Guardian of the Terridae despite—

The Terridae?

Dumarest felt the cold shock of belated recognition. The ending implied resemblance. An affinity with what went before. Terr. Terra?

The Terra was another name for Earth!

"Two minutes," said Volodya.

Dumarest ignored him as he considered the implications. The caskets decorated with their symbols; the signs of the zodiac which signposted Earth. Caskets used by the Terridae? Guarded by others of the same conviction?

Would Volodya willingly destroy his own?

"One minute," he said and Dumarest heard the sharp intake of Kusche's breath. The mutter of his barely vocalized prayer. "Fifty-five seconds." An eternity, and then, "I must insist on your answer."

Dumarest had to be correct or die. Killing as he died but tasting the bitter irony of losing what he had searched for so long to find in the final moment of success.

He said, "I do not beg for life—I demand you give it. Demand, too, your hospitality and protection—things it is your duty to provide. For I am of Earth." A pause then, in a tone which held the rolling pulses of drums, Dumarest continued, "From terror they fled to find new places on which to expiate their sins. Only when cleansed will the race of Man be again united."

The creed of the Original People—and his hope of life!

At his side Marya Seipolda said, "Earl, I'm the most fortunate girl here to have won you in the draw. I hope you don't mind."

A compliment which Dumarest returned, to be rewarded with a smile.

"Do you mind if I hold your arm? You're so tall, so hard and strong!" Her fingers rested like delicate petals on his sleeve. "Once, when I was very young, I knew a man like you. I forget his name but he was a technician. He died, I think. He must have died."

As she had lived, to walk now at his side, looking young and fragile, seeming almost to float as they walked down a corridor carpeted with soft green, the walls adorned with the depiction of shrubs and flowers and brightly winged butterflies. A scene in which she belonged; her face held the planes and lines of an elfin beauty, the lips small yet full, the jaw barely defined, the eyes too large beneath brows too high. Her hair was a skein of fine gold which rested like a delicate mist on her neatly rounded skull. An unformed face, as she had an unformed body. One looking as if fresh-made and waiting for the stamp of experience. It was hard to realize that she was three times his age.

"I hate the times of Waking," she said. "It's such a waste but the Elders insist on it. They say we have to exercise at times and renew our contact with reality. Such nonsense! Who wants reality when it is so much more fun to lie and dream? When the Event happens, of course, things will be different." A shadow marred the soft beauty of her face. "Will it happen soon, Earl? I've waited so long! Will it happen soon?"

The Event. The time when Earth would be discovered. The moment the Terridae waited for locked in the safe comfort of their caskets. A thing Volodya had explained as he had issued a warning.

"I must accept your claim but the final decision must rest with the Council. A keen mind, a lucky guess, a scrap of accidentally acquired knowledge—these things could mean little. But, in the meantime, you are free to enjoy Zabul."

A freedom curtailed by invisible bars; watchers who blocked passages, who steered him from one point to another with casual deftness. Jailers who, while always polite, were always at hand. Others had not been so reticent and Marya had been among them. Now, happy with her prize, she guided him to the great hall.

It held an assembly of ghosts.

They sat in a pale, blue light at long tables heaped with a variety of delicacies placed on salvers between flasks of scented wine. Their clothing was simple, lacking hard, strong colors: loose robes which masked their bodies and gave them a common appearance, enhanced by the impression of fragility, of age arrested, of life spent in small and measured doses. A blend of men and women covering a wide span of apparent age: dotards sitting with nymphs, striplings with crones. Their conversation rustled as if the words were brittle leaves stirred by the wind. Among them the Guardians looked like creatures of steel, men and women filled with the pulse of life, their eyes lacking the general vagueness, set on the present and not on some far distant future.

As Dumarest entered the hall one came toward him. She was tall, with a mane of burnished hair, the bright copper in strong contrast to the gossamer gray and silver white, the pale gold and amber, the delicate strands of black and brown borne by the Terridae.

"Earl Dumarest!" She held out her right hand, palm upward, smiling her pleasure as he touched it with his own. "The old greeting, I'm glad you know it. I'm Althea Hesford. What do you think of our world?"

He said dryly, "From the little I've seen of it, it seems an interesting place."

"A diplomat. You know how to be tactful. Urich said as much." She glanced at Marya. "Fydor has been looking for you, my dear. Why don't you join him?"

"I'm with Earl."

"You can see him later."

"But I won him!"

"He knows that. Do you want Fydor to be unhappy?" She smiled as the girl hurried away, losing the smile as she looked at Dumarest. "What do you think of our charges?"

"Entrancing."

"Unusual would be a better word." Her eyes hardened a little. "Why don't you say it?"

"Say it for me."

"They are too ignorant, too childish, too damned stupid and too damned weak. Right?"

Dumarest said mildly, "I would have called them innocent. Is that such a bad thing?"

"No, I guess not." Her eyes softened as again she smiled. "I think I like you, Earl Dumarest."

"And I you, Althea Hesford. Are you my new jailer?"

"Let's just say that I'm your companion. Have you eaten? Taken wine? Is there anything you would like to know that I can tell you? Above all I'd like for you to be comfortable and at ease."

"The condemned man was given a hearty breakfast," he said and explained as he saw the puzzlement in her eyes. "A custom on many worlds. A man due to be executed is given a final meal."

She thought about it for a moment then said, "A stupid custom. Why waste food on a man when it can do him no good?"

"Why be polite to someone you intend to kill?"

This time she needed no time for thought. "Earl, is that what you think? That we are going to destroy you? Surely Urich explained. You are to be tested, that is all. A formality to ensure you are what you claim to be. You can appreciate the reason. No Outsider can be tolerated here. Zabul is for the Terridae."

"And those who look after them?"

"Naturally. How could they survive without our protection?" She reached for a flask of wine, lifting it, setting it down as he shook his head. A salver of cakes followed as he again rejected the offering. "It's a question of finance," she continued. "Of maintenance and supply. Of increase, too, for it's impossible to breed while lying locked in boxes. We serve and we guard."

"From choice?" Dumarest saw the faint pucker between her brows. "Could you lie in a casket if you wanted?"

"Oh, I see what you mean." Her laughter held the amused innocence of a child. "Of course I could. In fact I have my own box and use it at times when in danger of getting bored. It's pleasant to lie and sleep and dream and wake feeling young and refreshed. One day I'll be like the others and stay longer in the casket. When I'm getting old and frightened of death. And it would be nice to witness the Event."

Nice?

To witness her millennium—nice?

A word she could have used because there was none to describe what the Terridae yearned to happen—or had the understatement been deliberate? Dumarest reached for a spiced morsel and turned to catch the emerald glint of her eyes beneath the arched copper of her brows, a shrewdness which dissolved into casual interest as he bit into the fragment.

"Nice? Try this, Earl." She lifted a decorated pot containing an aspic tinted a delicate pink and filled with segments of some sea creature. "Mordon," she explained. "An eel which lurks in deep water among fissured rocks. Its bite can kill."

"So you have oceans on Zabul?"

"We have everything the universe can provide on Zabul." Again he caught her watchful, calculating glance. "Everything but the most important. That can only come from one place."

"Earth."

"Of course." She ate a portion of eel with the neat fastidiousness of a feline and waited until he had finished his own. "More? No? You are wise. To gain maximum enjoyment it is best to sample as wide a variety as possible and not to become replete on a single item." She moved down the table, looking, touching, finally selecting a small cone which, when broken, emitted an acrid perfume. "Ghanga buds," she explained. "Their perfume cleans the palate and sharpens the appetite." She proffered the bowl and set it down as Dumarest shook his head. "Do I bore you?"

"No."

"You mean that?"

He said, "Novelty is never boring and, to me, you are novel."

"As you are to me, Earl. There is so much I want to ask you. So many things I want to talk about. Later, perhaps?"

"Why not now?"

"There isn't time." She echoed a genuine regret. "I have to take you before the Council."

Chapter Nine

They sat around a table in a long, low chamber decorated with a frieze of running animals, all in softly glowing colors. Diffused lighting softened their faces, blurring the sharply etched lines of age, the sunken eyes, the mouths grown taut with the passing of years. Among them Urich Volodya looked young, Althea little more than a child. Dumarest could almost smell the dust of antiquity.

Vole opened the proceedings. He sat hunched in his chair, the plate resting before him bearing his name. One name, and the plate was matched by others, each before a figure in a chair. Dumarest wondered at the need—had their memories grown so unreliable? Or did they, as did so many others exercising authority, believe that to be harsh and Spartan was to be efficient?

"We the Council of Zabul and the Guardians of the Terridae are assembled to determine the truth of your claim to be of Earth." Vole had a voice which matched his face: thin, dry, the words sharply delineated. "Althea Hesford will act as your adviser and explain any points of which you may be in doubt. You know the penalty should we not be satisfied."

Dumarest said flatly, "Why do you think I am lying?"

"That charge has not been made."

"Yet it is implied. This assembly is proof of that." Dumarest glanced from one to the other. "You believe in the existence of Earth but I have no need of belief. I know it is no legend. I know it is real. I know—you understand? I *know!*"

Gouzh said dryly, "We of the Guardians are not as inexperienced as our charges. We know that attack is often the best form of defense."

"I was not making an attack but stating my position."

"Even so, flat statements mean little. It is best to examine the evidence piece by piece. Tell us of the Original People."

A test—they must know the answer; Volodya's forbearance was proof of that.

Without hesitation Dumarest said, "They are a sect of minor importance to be found on various planets. They cultivate secrecy and neither seek nor welcome converts. The main tenet of their belief is that Mankind originated on a single world, Earth, and that after cleansing by tribulation the race will return to the world of its origin." He added, "I could give you greater detail but would prefer not to."

"Why? Are you of them?"

"I was accepted by them."

"And wish to respect their confidence." A woman, Logan, spoke from where she sat. "Do you follow their belief?" Her voice sharpened as he made no answer. "Do you?"

A trap? Did they adhere to the same faith? On the face of it, even to surmise that all the widespread branches of the human race could have originated on one, single world was ridiculous. Environment governed appearance, together with genetic mutation, and how could black and brown, yellow and copper and white, all have shared the same air, the same sun?

Althea came to his rescue. She said, "Earl Dumarest is not being tested as to his beliefs but for the truth of his claim regarding his planet of origin."

"A good point." Haren backed her objection. "We must be fair." To Dumarest he said, "What proof have you that you were born on Earth, as you claim?"

"What proof will you accept? The verdict of a lie-detector? If so I am willing to cooperate in such interrogation."

Logan said quietly, "The results may not be conclusive. A man convinced he is telling the truth will register as truthful. That is not to say the truth is what he claims."

"Conditioning? Delusion?" Haren frowned and glanced at Volodya. "Is it possible?"

Gouzh spoke before Volodya could reply. "Of course it is! Logan is right—and remember it was Dumarest himself who suggested the test. To me this is indicative of the fact he knows he must pass it. In turn this could mean he has been prepared for such an examination. My vote is—"

"There will be no vote!" Volodya spoke for the first time. "This assembly will be conducted according to established precedent. Only after a full investigation has been made will a decision be reached." He added coldly, "I suggest that certain members of the Council should strive for greater objectivity."

They accepted that rebuke but Dumarest wondered if there had been more. A warning? Subtle advice for him to be careful? Already he had sensed the hostility where he had anticipated interest. The woman's objection to a lie-detector examination—sophistry, but why? Why?

"A point baffles me." Another woman from lower down the table broke the silence. Tilsey—younger than Logan but with eyes as hard, lips as set, mind as unyielding. "You claim to have been born on Earth, left it when young and now wish to return. I fail to see the difficulty. Surely, if you left it, you must know where it is."

An obvious question but one holding undertones, and Dumarest hesitated before answering. To lie? To claim he possessed the coordinates? On the face of it they should welcome him for having ushered in the Event, but he felt the old, familiar tension preceding danger. A warning he had long since learned never to ignore. It would be safer to tell the truth.

"My lady, I know it exists."

"That is not answering the question."

"No," admitted Dumarest. "I find it hard to answer."

"Try," whispered Althea. "Try!"

He took the advice, knowing his life hung in the balance.

"I was very young," he said. "A mere boy, little more than a child. My parents were dead and I'd been taken in by others. We argued and I left home. After a long journey I stumbled on a ship with strange markings. I stowed away."

To crouch cold and terrified in a darkened corner, afraid to move, afraid even to breathe, waiting as he forced trembling limbs to be still, fighting cramps and the pains of hunger. Tasting bile from nausea and blood from his bitten lips. Things he didn't mention, as he had glossed over the rest. Leaving out the blood, the death and pain, the savage violence of his childhood world.

"I was lucky," he continued. "The captain was old and kind, in his fashion. He could have evicted me but he let me work my passage. I stayed with him until he died."

To be stranded on a hostile world. A stranger bereft of the protection of House or Guild or Family. To survive as best he could and to move on. To plunge deeper into the heart of the galaxy where suns were close and worlds plentiful. To where Earth was nothing but the stuff of legend.

"Is that all?" Haren cleared his throat. "Is that all you care to tell us?"

"There has to be more." Vole was emphatic. "There has to be. Why are you so reticent?"

Dumarest said, "When I tried to find Earth again it was impossible to discover the coordinates. The old captain would have known them but he was dead and his log lost or destroyed. No almanac lists them, no navigational tables—but you know this!"

"Yes," said Vole. "We know. The location of Earth is a mystery yet to be resolved. But one thing is clear beyond question—you do not come from Earth."

"You say I lie?"

"Did you see the soaring towers of crystal? The floating cities? The tremendous waterfalls which contain all the colors of the universe and shake the air with celestial music? The trees on which grow a score of various fruits and nuts and flowers together with scented and succulent leaves? The pools in which, once immersed, a man grows younger again and a woman more beautiful? Did you talk with the Shining Ones and learn of their esoteric lore? Walk in endless caverns of awesome majesty? Know the end of pain and hunger and need? The cessation of fear?" He leaned forward, eyes burning with a febrile light. "Are you immortal?"

"No," said Dumarest. "I am not that."

"Then you cannot be of Earth. Not the Earth we seek and the finding of which will herald the Event. You come from some small backward planet, perhaps. One aspiring to greatness by the local use of a hallowed name, but that can be all." Vole raised a hand to still any protest. "The Council has heard enough. Leave. When we have decided your fate you will be notified."

As usual the room had been tidied, the beds made, fresh

wine set together with a tray of delicacies on the table. Acts performed by invisible servants or by those who watched his every move. Dumarest closed the door behind him and leaned back against it as he looked at the furnishings. They, like the beds, the cushions and carpet on the floor, were soft and luxurious but, even so, the place was a cell.

One he was, as yet, permitted to leave, but how long would that freedom last?

The door was a smooth panel broken only by the orifice of a thumb-operated latch. It could be locked only from the outside. Dumarest stooped, lifted the knife from his boot and rammed the blade beneath the lower edge. Acting as a wedge it would hold the door against intrusion. Rising, he again examined the room.

The beds stood on short legs, the pneumatic mattresses covered with light sheets of gaily decorated plastic. His own was nearest to the door and he moved forward to stand beside the other. Nubar Kusche was absent, engaged in business of his own, maintaining a low profile as he sheltered beneath Dumarest's wing.

Quickly Dumarest searched his bed, turning over the mattress, the stand itself, running his fingers over every inch. He found nothing and moved on, checking his own bed, the table, the chairs, probing the cushions and examining the underside of the carpet. In the bathroom he continued the search. The door to the room in which he had wakened was still locked and he examined the panel. Back in the other room he knelt and checked the position of his knife. None seemed to have tried the door. Jerking free the blade, he sheathed it and lay supine on his bed.

And heard again the music of dreams.

He turned, listening, trying to localize the sounds. They were small, a susurration which held within itself a medley of notes and chords and sequences all pitched in a close-to-subaudible murmur. Ghosts whispering in nighted graveyards as they bewailed lost opportunities and vain regrets. The unborn whimpering as they feared the harsh expulsion from the snug comfort of the womb. The thin echoes of fear and the shadows of joy.

Against the tips of his fingers the wall felt hard and cold.

He turned again to look at the ceiling, which spread like a nacreous cloud from wall to wall. A seemingly unbroken expanse but if Volodya had spoken the truth it would mask watching eyes and things which could do more than watch—an electronic guard system with lasers following the radiated heat of his body or directed jets of nerve gas which could drop him in screaming agony.

What would the Council decide?

Vole was easy to predict, Logan too; both had revealed a bigoted mind. Had he argued, they would have destroyed him for his heresy in threatening their faith in an idealized concept of Earth. The others? He looked at their faces, delineated by memory against the expanse of the ceiling. Gouzh, Haren, Volodya, others. Tilsey might be an ally, though a weak one, yet her vote could soften the verdict. Volodya had seemed sympathetic, and Demich, who had said nothing, had nodded encouragement. Individuals who could be swayed by a majority, but who, in turn, could force that majority to be less adamant.

And he had not lied—none could accuse him of that.

Had Kusche?

Dumarest, of necessity, traveled light. The entrepreneur had no such pressure, yet he had no baggage, nothing but his clothes and the deck of cards and the jewelry on his person: the heavy-stoned ring, a thin chain of gold rings carried around his neck, a bracelet on his left wrist. Portable wealth, a part of any mercenary's normal garb and an elementary precaution for anyone who lived by his wits on the edge of danger.

A man who had left a safe world on the thin chance of gain.

How much did he know?

Dumarest turned again, restless, feeling the prickle which warned of danger. The room was a trap, as was the building, the situation into which he had been thrown. One compounded by those who ruled Zabul and who even now could have condemned him to death. Yet this trap held an irresistible bait—here, if anywhere, he must surely find the clues which would guide him to Earth.

The sound of the door brought him to his feet, carried him to the panel, the knife in his hand, steel gleaming as it rose to come to rest.

"Earl?" Kusche swallowed, moving back from the blade

which had halted against his throat. "What the hell's come over you?"

"Nothing. Forget it. Where have you been?"

"Moving around, talking, learning what I could. It was little enough. What did the Council decide?"

"They're still deciding. They'll let us know."

"You, Earl, not me. I abrogated my responsibility. What they decide for you will apply to me also." Kusche moved deeper into the room and stood looking down at the table with its wine and delicacies. "They're mad, all of them. Living in this maze like rats in a warren. A pity we learned too late. The chance of a lifetime and we didn't know." He poured himself wine as if yielding to an inward struggle. "And it would have been so easy."

Dumarest watched the entrepreneur as he drank. The man seemed to have shrunken a little, lost some of his oozing confidence, his easy bonhomie. Now, as he swallowed the wine, little points of reflected brilliance danced from the stone of his heavy ring.

"A chance," he said again as he set down the goblet. "You to make the claim and me to back you. You know the game as well as I do. Tell them what they want to hear. Embroider it as much as the traffic will stand and arouse their hope and greed. Sell them something you haven't got, then make them afraid of losing what they never had. Promises, speculations, hints—there would have been no need of lies. You could have given them what they wanted and named your own price."

The location of Earth. The thing he didn't have. Dryly, Dumarest mentioned it.

"You could have invented something, Earl. Fed them a line. Hell, this is no time to grow a conscience. Not when our lives are at stake."

A man in character, putting the question of easy profit first, the regret at a lost opportunity, mentioning personal danger only at the end. An act? If so he performed well—but light sparkled from the quiver of his ring as he poured himself more wine.

Dumarest left him to it, stepping from the room into the passage outside, to stand for a moment with his fingers resting on the wall, to turn finally to his right where stairs rose in sweeping curves to the upper galleries.

She came to him while he sat on a bench studying a mural depicting a wooded glade, halting to one side as her eyes searched his face. A scrutiny he ignored as she slowly came close, rising when her hand touched his shoulder to turn and look down into the wide-spaced green eyes inches below his own.

"Althea?"

Her name and a question which she chose to leave unanswered.

"You knew I was there," she accused. "How?"

"I smelled your perfume."

"I don't wear any."

"The scent of your hair," he said, and touched it with a gentle hand. "The Council?"

"Have made their decision." He was in no mood for games and she had been at fault to tease him. "You are to be given a choice, Earl, but I know which you will take. To stay here and work with us. To mingle with us and to join us in every way."

"As an equal?"

"In time, yes." Then as she saw his expression she added quickly, "You must be fair. You came here as an uninvited stranger. An interloper. The trespass alone merited death. You are still an unknown quality. After a few years in which to prove your loyalty you will become truly one of the Terridae."

And, until then, to do what? Dumarest could guess the answer. No establishment such as he had seen could operate without those to tend the machines, clean the halls, dust, sweep, clean. He would live as a menial.

"And the alternative?"

"One you would not accept. Death, Earl." Her hand rested on his own, her fingers warm, groping with a sudden intimacy. "Don't let's talk about it."

"Why not? Are you afraid of death?" She and all the rest of the Terridae, and he saw the movement of her eyes, the small signs which betrayed her fear of personal termination. More gently he said, "All things die in their season, Althea. It is the way of life—as you must know to have depicted it so well."

He turned her to face the mural, pointing out the drift of gaudy-winged insects, the birds waiting to feed on the bright allure, the faint mesh of a spider's web, the furry creature watching the bird as it was watched in turn by a lithe animal larger than itself.

A lesson in paint wrought with artistic genius like those he had seen repeated over and over in the corridors and chambers of galleries: adornment enamored of life, each wall a canvas for its depiction.

She said, "Earl! You're hurting me!"

"Sorry."

He released his grip but the pressure of his fingers remained on her arm to stir her senses with ghostly dominance. An unconscious display of his strength and she felt the reaction of her body in a flood of raw and primitive demand, which she resisted with the aid of banal conversation.

"We love life," she explained, looking at the mural and feeling it necessary to explain. "Death is so final. A total erasure. A waste." Pausing, she added, "That's why some of us wanted our caskets decorated. A fashion I think will be discontinued. At least the habit of using outside artists. The pursuit of perfection can be carried too far."

"Is your casket decorated?"

"Of course. Would you like to see it?" She stepped from him to turn, smiling, waiting for him to follow. "It isn't far."

She led him to an elevator which dropped them to lower depths where the air held a chill crispness and thick padding muffled their footsteps as it absorbed echoes, turning her words into a flat monotone. Chatter to which he paid little attention, concentrating instead on the chambers with their low roofs and thick dividing walls, the caskets set out in neat array.

"Here!" She halted beside one, turning to look at him with a smile. "What do you think of it?"

She raised the lid, a portion of the side swinging down to allow easy examination and entry. Within, the padding was of pale green, the carvings the deeper hue of natural jade. Again they depicted life but were subtly different from those he had seen in the other box. The figures were less polished, less discreet in shape and form and action. As she grew older they would probably be changed but now, in her, the tide of life and creation ran strong.

"It's snug," she said from where she stood at his side. "Warm and cozy. Once the lid is down nothing else matters, nothing else exists."

And nothing would be lacking except the one thing she now needed. Dumarest could sense it; the femininity she radiated, which carried her sexual invitation and desire. A message of which she was consciously unaware but which betrayed her inner yearnings.

"Earl!" Her hand was warm against his own. "Would you like to try it? With me, I mean? There is room for us both."

To lie and yield to the pleasure of the moment, to feel the softness of her, to respond to her passion. Time extended by the magic contained in the casket, minutes turned into hours, hours into days. A time to dream and sleep, to dream and wake to dream again. Time flowing past like a streaming river. Time he did not have.

"Earl?" Her hand closed in anticipation of his answer. "Will you go first?"

"No." He softened his refusal. "This isn't the time, Althea."

She misunderstood, the false explanation saving her from the hurt of rejection.

"Of course! You're worried about the verdict. But, Earl, you have no choice. To die or to work with us—how can you hesitate?"

The logic of a child; she hadn't even considered the other alternative. To die or to stay, she had said—what if he chose to leave?

A question he almost asked, then changed his mind as caution prickled its warning. As yet she was friendly, almost an ally; it would be madness to make her an enemy. And he could guess the answer: if he tried to leave they would kill him. At least they would try.

He stepped back, looking at her casket, memorizing the decorations, the small differences which distinguished it from the others. So many others. He counted them, added the number of rooms he had seen, guessed at others which must exist. When had it begun?

"A long time ago, Earl," she said when, later, he put the question. "A thousand years at least. Maybe two—I'm not sure."

"Who would know?"

"The Elders, perhaps. The Archives. Does it matter?"

She had taken him to a small park which rested beneath a domed roof flushed with the gold and amber of a summer's day. The place held the soft music of running water, the air heavy with the scent of flowers. Listening, Dumarest could hear the faint susurration of voices as some of the Terridae sat and conversed in private conference.

Men and women renewing their contact with reality, Althea had said, but for them this reality was no more substantial than a dream.

"So many questions, Earl," she whispered. "So many thoughts. I can see them crossing your mind. But why bother? Given time all will be clear. Why not just enjoy the moment? Don't you like it here?"

He said, "Do you like the shape of mountains? To climb up high among the snow and ice? To swim in tepid seas and to run in one straight line as if you were an arrow aimed at the horizon?"

"Of course! In dreams—"

"In reality," he interrupted. "To do these things not dream about them. To scratch a foot and feel the pain as you see the blood. To stand and fill your lungs with air so cold it hurts. To dive so deep your ears feel as if they must burst, then to rise and break surface and to see the sun gilding the waves. To feel. To know hate and love and fear. To know pain. To know happiness, to laugh and, yes, to cry also. Life, girl! I'm talking about life!"

Real life, not the stuff of dreams, the kind she had never experienced and so could never fully understand. But that, at least, she could change.

Chapter Ten

----·×·——·×·——·×·----

The room was a place of scents and dusty shadows; a pale illumination from concealed lights threw bizarre silhouettes against walls and ceiling—the shapes of monsters and beasts and watchful birds of prey all born from small ornaments and crumpled fabrics; the slender grace of a statuette, the squat form of a beaming idol. The things belonged to the woman as did most of the odors, and Dumarest caught the scent of the perfume of her body and hair. Caught too the natural exudations of consummated passion common to them both.

Beside him on the wide bed Althea stirred and moved to place a hand on his naked torso, her own resting with febrile softness against his arm. In the pale illumination she seemed fashioned of marble, the contours of her face veiled by the profusion of her hair.

A woman in love or one who had claimed to be. Certainly one of passion and savage demand. Now, satiated, she snuggled against him lost in a natural sleep.

Dumarest wondered if she dreamed.

For him there had been no dreams, no sleep either, though he had forced himself to rest. Now he glanced again at the room and its furnishings, assessing them, setting them against their owner. Althea's things, each a reflection of her personality. The statuette was that of a woman, arms uplifted, face upturned, her entire body shaped in an attitude of desperate yearning. The idol squatted and smiled. A flask held a temporary forgetfulness, and a transparent box held a dried flower together with a scatter of seeds.

Wanting, patience, the belief in resurrection. Death followed by rebirth—the symbolism of the flower and seeds was obvious. As was the wine—blood of the fruits of the earth.

Earth!

Rising from sleep, Althea felt the tension of his body. "Earl," she murmured. "Earl."

"It's all right." His hand touched her hair. "Go back to sleep."

She sighed, trying to obey, and his hand lingered on the thick, copper tresses. Her hair was like that of Earth or as close to the planet as anyone he had ever met and at least they had that in common. Yet the Earth she dreamed of was not the world he knew. The Terridae imagined a planet of endless splendors: or, a virtual paradise which would be theirs to enjoy once found. The Event which would terminate their present mode of existence.

"Earl?" She moved again, her hand sliding over his chest, the fingers following the tracery of thin scars which marred his torso, scars which were the medals won in early combats when, to survive, he had to deal death or be killed. "Earl?"

She snuggled closer as he caressed her hair, almost fully awake now, but content just to lie and remember the passion which had dominated her, the fury of biological need which had held them in an old and pleasant madness.

"What are you thinking of, darling?"

"You." A lie but not wholly so. "Earth."

"Not these?" Her fingers moved over the pattern of cicatrices. "How did you get them, darling? Some wild beast?"

More than one and they had been the most savage form of life ever created. Predators on two legs armed with razor-edged steel. Men determined to kill. He had been one of them, faster than the others, more intent on survival, just that little extra lucky. Facts proved by his continued existence.

"Earl?"

"Go to sleep."

She wouldn't obey but lay quietly as he stroked her hair, and against the ceiling he could see the reflected images her words had aroused. Memories which filled the chamber with the sight and sound of beasts; the stinks, the remembered tensions. Even as he watched, the bizarre shadows became a ring of staring faces blotched with avid eyes. Men and women, the rich and supposedly cultured, screaming as they demanded blood and pain. Taking a vicarious pleasure from the spectacle of two men fighting to the death with naked blades. Betting, cursing, touching hysteria as the madness gripped them.

The arena!

The means by which he had kept himself alive, and he thought again of the burning wounds, the blood, the fear, the pain of his younger days. The school in which he had refined hard-won skills and learned that to hesitate was to die. Learned too the necessity of relying on no one but himself.

The images dissolved and turned back into bizarre shadows and Dumarest realized he had slipped over the edge into sleep. The woman had gone but from the adjoining bathroom came the sound of gushing water. Althea entered the bedroom as he rose, smiling her pleasure at seeing him awake.

"You looked so peaceful, darling. I hadn't the heart to wake you."

"A kindness to match your beauty."

"Flatterer!" She turned from him, swirling her robe and the mane of fresh-washed copper hair, but the compliment had pleased her. "Do you really think I'm beautiful?"

"Ask your mirror."

"I don't care what my mirror thinks." She faced him, smiling, her eyes luminous. "But you, Earl, that's different. What you think matters."

"I think you are beautiful."

"Darling!"

He touched the hands she extended toward him and stood for a moment meeting the direct stare of her eyes. Then, without comment, he turned and headed toward the shower and the artificial rain which thundered down with heat and cold to lave the residue of passion from his body and the drifting vestiges of sleep from his mind.

Hot air dried him and a rough towel provided a stimulating friction. With it wrapped around his waist he returned to the bedroom, where Althea leaned supine on the wide couch, her robe parted to display the long smooth curve of her thigh. An invitation he ignored.

"Earl?" She frowned as he began to dress. "What are you doing, darling?"

"I'm going to find a window."

THE TERRIDAE   103

"A what!" Astonishment brought her up from the bed. "Earl, are you serious?"

"Very." His tone left her in no doubt. "I want to see the sun, the land, the sky." The field if there was one and the ships on it. The way of escape, if escape was possible, which he doubted. Things he didn't mention as, again, he said, "I just want to find a window. You could save me time by taking me to one."

"I can't!" She slumped to sit on the edge of the bed. "It isn't possible. Earl—please!"

He looked at her, seeing her pleading expression, lifting his eyes to look around the chamber, at the solid walls decorated with the usual theme. As all walls were solid. In all he had seen of Zabul there had been no trace of a window and he could guess the reason.

The girl would help him verify it.

Althea said dully, "This is the best I can do, Earl, and I've done too much. No Outsider should learn what you have or see what you are to see now. I must be mad to cooperate."

But he had encouraged this madness, turning her passion against her conditioning and making her his ally as she had made him her lover. Now he watched as she manipulated dials and paused with her hand on a contact. A moment and it was done.

Dumarest stared at the naked glory of space.

He had seen it before yet, always, it thrilled. The countless stars with their hosts of worlds, the blotches of darkness, the blurred patches which were other galaxies, the whole, incredible vastness of the universe. Then the scene changed as the scanner turned to portray Zabul.

A ship, as he had suspected, but gigantic in size.

Yet—was it a ship?

The form was wrong, the shape and balance, the beauty of functional design. There were too many towers, too many vanes and bulbous swellings and shadowed declivities. It was as if a giant had assembled scores of vessels and welded them into a shape dictated by whimsical chance, joining the hulls with sheets of curved metal, extra bubbles, scraps which had been ready at hand, expanding the original concept in dimensions determined by need and available material.

Dumarest said, "How long?"

"I don't know, Earl. I told you that. I was born on Zabul and to me it has always been home. My world. One I have betrayed."

"No."

"Because you guessed? How?"

"Vibration," he said. "And other things." His instinct mostly; he had traveled on too many ships not to be sensitive to space. But the vibrations had triggered his suspicions: the blur of sounds which had come to him as music. On any isolated structure trapped noises tended to travel, to become amplified, to linger in telltale whisperings. "But you haven't betrayed anything. Others must know of Zabul. The Huag-Chi-Tsacowa, for example. And what of your other suppliers?"

She said, "You're just trying to be kind. No matter what you say, I have broken a trust. The Elders—"

"To hell with them!"

It would have been kinder to have slapped her in the face. She recoiled, eyes haunted, her hand shaking as she broke the connection. The screen went blank and a panel slid over it to turn it back into a part of a decorated wall that formed a small chamber fitted with chairs—part of an upper gallery.

Dumarest said, "You prate of finding Earth but what do you hope to find there? One thing must be freedom or all else is valueless. Why be afraid of the Elders? What are they but people who have clung to power for too long? Old, decaying, almost senile, close to being insane. Have spirit, Althea. Life is not to be lived in chains."

"No, Earl! You don't understand!"

He shrugged and looked at the panel covering the screen, the wall, the chairs set in neat array. An auditorium designed for a forgotten purpose or, perhaps, those for whom it had been built were no longer interested.

Quietly he said, "How did it all begin? Did the younger sons of some rich families unite in a common aim? Or did the rulers of some commercial empire look for a way to extend their lives and power? It's happened often in the course of history: those with wealth and authority chafing with the need to attend to every small detail. They hire or promote others to take over the worry of day-to-day business and turn to other, more enjoyable pursuits. But no matter what the reason, the result is always the same. Once power is yielded it is lost. Those promoted to handle the finances are reluctant to relinquish their positions. Normally it doesn't matter; those who have yielded their fight are too busy having pleasure, and they die before managing to disturb the existing state of affairs. But if they should live too long—what then, Althea?"

"What?" She blinked as if recapturing her thoughts. "I don't understand."

"I think you do. The Guardians—such a well-chosen word. The elect who look after those in the caskets and take care of all the tiresome details. What was it you told me? All the fruits of the universe come to Zabul—but who pays the price?"

"We help," she said. "Someone has to take care of things. The Guardians do good."

"Yes," he said dryly. "They do good. In fact they do very well."

She caught the tone, the meaning, the implied insult, and her hand rose, fingers curved, nails aimed to rip at his cheek. But her blow died as he gripped her wrist to hold it, staring into her eyes.

"Do you really want to find Earth?"

"How can you doubt it?"

"Do they? The Council?"

"Of course!" She winced and pulled at her wrist. Her hand had grown white beneath the pressure of his fingers. "Earl! My hand!"

"I come from Earth," he said as he released her. "By any form of logic here is a place where I surely should be welcome. To be questioned, tested, probed—at least to be listened to. Yet what happened? You were at the meeting and saw how they reacted."

"So?"

"They don't want to find Earth."

"Impossible! They, all of us, live only for the Event!"

"So they tell you and so you believe." Dumarest hammered the point. "But think of how they reacted, what they said and did, their final decision. I offered to be tested and was refused—can you agree with the logic of that decision?"

"Logan had her reasons."

"And her fears. What happens to the Council after the Event? Who will give the orders? Fill the seats of power? You have everything the universe can provide," he said bitterly. "Maybe some of the Council have developed expensive tastes."

"No!"

"Think about it. How can you be certain that I was not sent to examine you? To gauge your fitness to experience the Event. The one chance you will ever have, Althea. Thrown away by the greed of those who claim to rule you. Think about it, damn you! Think!"

Think and let the seeds of doubt he had planted sprout and grow into mistrust and suspicion. It was the only chance he had. To destroy the rule of the Council in order to gain his own freedom—from more than their decree. Zabul was a ship and, if he had been traced, was now a prison.

"Earl?" Her tone was pleading as were her eyes. "Help me, darling."

To think? No, it was more than that and he was suddenly conscious of her vulnerability. Sheltered from childhood, protected, raised in a culture which admitted of no question as to its destiny, fed on dreams in which no unpleasantness could exist—how could she be other than a victim of those used to the normal rigors of life? The cheating and lying and violence and mistrust which all took in from their earliest days. Assimilated it and learned to live with it.

And, like her, the Council.

"You must spread the word," he said. "To Volodya and Demich and those others who were more open-minded than Vole and the rest. Talk to them. Mention the chance they could be losing. Demand I be treated as what I am—the true representative of Earth. Unless you can demonstrate your desire for freedom you are not worthy of the Event."

Alone, he reactivated the screen, operating the controls she had touched and which he'd memorized. The stars were in their same, eternal splendor but his eyes shadowed as he looked at the spaces between.

How long did he have before the enemy would strike?

Nubar Kusche woke from a dream in which all he touched turned to precious metal to stare into the face hovering above his own.

"Earl!" He tried to rise, then fell back as something pricked his throat. Dabbing it, he saw a smear of blood on his fingers. "Earl, for God's sake!"

Dumarest lifted the knife to hold it poised in his right hand, his forearm resting on his knee, his right foot on the edge of Kusche's bed.

He said mildly, "It's time we had a talk."

"At the point of a knife?"

"Anyway you want—as long as you tell me the truth." The blade shifted, catching the light, reflecting it, forming transient glitters. "We'll start with Caval. Why did you ride with the casket?"

"I told you."

"Tell me again." Dumarest listened, waiting until Kusche had finished. "You're lying. I want the truth."

"You've had it." Kusche dabbed at his face, at his neck, looking at the sweat now mixed with the blood. "I just thought we could make a deal."

"You're an entrepreneur," said Dumarest. "Not a gambler. You look for the chance to make an easy profit. The opportunity others may have missed or the opportunity you can make. Nothing wrong in that unless you come up against someone with strong objections to be used. I'm that kind of person." The knife dipped, light gleaming on curved edges and point. "Who contacted you on Caval and told you to watch me?"

"No one. I swear it!"

"And later?" Dumarest's voice hardened. "The truth, you fool!"

"Earl—"

"You were contacted and offered a commision, which you accepted. Ride with the casket—and what?"

"Nothing." Kusche lifted a defensive hand as he saw Dumarest's expression. "For God's sake, it's the truth! I was just to ride with you."

"As you are? What about your baggage?"

"I had a valise and a kitbag. I lost them both." Kusche scowled. "There were some good things in that baggage: deeds to productive mines on nearby worlds, some samples, the formula of a new fuel. And I had a dozen good carvings, each worth a month's high living in the right market."

"And your pay?" Dumarest saw the flicker of the other's eyes. "Give it to me."

"Hell, man, it's all I've got!"

"You've a choice," said Dumarest. "I'm not playing games. You hand it over or I'll cut it from your finger." He held out his left hand as Kusche pulled free the ring with the heavy stone. "That's better. Now let's take a look inside."

Rising, he went into the bathroom, set the ring on the tiles and smashed the pommel of his knife against the stone. It yielded at the second blow and from the crystalline shards he picked out a thread of wire-mesh, some nodules almost too small to see and a pile of paper-thin wafers of metal a fraction of an inch across.

"The bastard!" Kusche stared from over Dumarest's shoulder. "He told me it was real. A genuine stone."

"Who?"

"Brice Quimper. He's an agent on Caval. Works for the Vosburgh Consortium." Kusche stared at the broken mechanism. "What was it?"

"A locator." Dumarest threw the scraps into the drain. "I guessed you must have had one and searched the room. When I couldn't find it I knew you had to be carrying it."

"Why?" Kusche answered his own question. "No baggage. But why?"

"Someone wanted to know just where you were at all times."

"Quimper?" Kusche frowned, then shook his head. If he was playing a part he was doing it well. "No—what reason could he have? I'm not important to him. I'm not important to anyone so—" He broke off, looking at Dumarest. "Not me, Earl—you! They wanted me to ride with you so as to know where you could be found."

"They?"

"Whoever it was used Quimper. What interest could he have in you? There has to be someone else. I suspected it when I saw the activity of the guards." Kusche frowned again. "Used," he said bitterly. "The bastards used me. Took my gear and damned near cost me my life." He rubbed at his throat. "If it hadn't been for your fast talk we could both be dead by now."

Which meant that someone had made a mistake and the Cyclan did not make mistakes. What then? Dumarest walked back into the other room, frowning, reviewing each moment since his waking. The casket—had a cyber predicted he was inside or had it been a lucky guess? The latter, he decided; for some reason no cyber had been present on Caval during his stay. If one had he would have been taken. Instead their agent had used his initiative and taken an inexpensive precaution. Kusche had just been a convenient tool—or was that just what he wished to appear?

Dumarest watched as the man crossed to the table and poured himself wine. The hand holding the decanter seemed steady enough now that there was no ring to betray small quivers, but the wine gurgled in an uneven stream.

"Earl?" Kusche shrugged as Dumarest shook his head. "Just as you want." He drank and lowered the goblet to take a deep breath. Naked aside from shorts, he had a smooth plumpness which matched his face but, Dumarest knew, most of the bulk was muscle.

He said, "How did you get knocked out?"

"On the way here? With gas, I think. Yes, it must have been gas." Kusche swallowed more wine. "One second I was in my bunk and the next I was here with Volodya standing over me." He added shrewdly, "Someone didn't want me around."

Or had wanted him to stay with the casket. The Huag-Chi-Twacowa? It was possible; they would not want to run foul of the Cyclan, and by gassing and transshipping Kusche they would have protected their employers and so served both masters. Had the Cyclan known of the transshipment? Did Kusche know he was not on a world?

He gulped when Dumarest told him and poured himself more wine. An act to gain time in which to compose himself or to arrange his thoughts.

"You're hotter than I guessed, Earl. I figured you for someone of value and hoped to make a deal but I never guessed at anything like this. Can you imagine what it takes to manipulate the Huag-Chi-Tsacowa? To fix it with them that I should be sent with the casket?" He looked at his bare finger. "Now we know why it had to be that way. Just who the hell is after you?"

"The Cyclan."

"What?"

"The Cyclan," repeated Dumarest and added, "Don't you want to know why?"

A temptation and he watched as Kusche tried to fight it. Knowledge was always an advantage; sometimes it could mean power and often meant wealth. At times, also, it could invite destruction.

"I've a secret," said Dumarest. "One stolen from the Cyclan. They want it back. They want it so badly they will give a fortune to the man who will deliver me unharmed into their hands. They will spend anything to make sure I'm captured. Do you understand?"

Kusche swallowed, his eyes wary. "Why tell me all this?"

"You wanted to be my friend. My partner." Dumarest crossed to the table and cleared it, then, with a finger dipped in wine, marked fifteen of the deck of cards with as many different symbols. Laying them out he said, "Look at them. Remember them. They read from left to right and you start at the top. Look at them!"

Kusche looked at his face, at the hand, which had dipped to touch the hilt of the knife, and reluctantly obeyed.

"Each symbol represents a biological molecular unit," said Dumarest. "The secret lies in the sequence of their arrangement. Now you know it. Now you are as important to the Cyclan as I am."

"No! How can I remember this?"

"Just keep looking."

At the cards, the symbols he had drawn on them, the components of the affinity twin. The discovery the Cyclan hunted him to regain, for with it they would have the means to dominate the galaxy. But Kusche did not share the secret; the cards he studied had been laid out at random. The symbols they carried were known to the Cyclan but the all-important sequence remained with Dumarest alone.

Something Kusche couldn't know. As he turned, his face beaded with sweat, Dumarest said, "Now we're really partners, Nubar. If I'm caught and handed over to the Cyclan I'll give them just five words. I'll say, 'Nubar Kusche knows the secret.' Can you guess what will happen then?"

He would be hunted in turn, taken, put to the question. He had seen the symbols and could never honestly deny it, and the Cyclan would ruin his body and brain to learn the order in which they had been displayed. And, even if they had gained the secret, still he would be destroyed.

"You bastard! You've given me nothing and put my head in a noose! Why do this to me?" Kusche reached for wine, his hand trembling. "Why?"

Dumarest said flatly, "Because I need your help."

Chapter Eleven

———◆◆◆———

Zabul was a world of spaces and each space was a world. Realms of diverse color: blue and green and burning crimson. Gold and white and soft lavender. In a bubble of emerald and azure Byrnne Vole sat and scowled at depictions of fish and weed, of tentacled shapes blurred by artistry and shells which rested like jewels on stones and gritty sand. A scene meant to give peace, but he was far from calm.

"It must be stopped!" His hand beat a soft tattoo on the table at which he sat. "This talk is dangerous! The man must be controlled. Althea Hesford—you are failing in your duty!"

She stood before the table, looking down at Vole, Logan, Gouzh and others. Demich, to one side, had smiled a greeting as she had entered the chamber and Volodya had worn his usual mask. Haren was absent, running back to the snug comfort of his casket, but the man who had taken his place could have been his twin.

Now Rhion said. "I have been briefed on the situation. To cast blame at this time would be useless but the handling of the matter leaves much to be desired. The responsibility is yours, Urich Volodya."

"To murder without trial?"

"What? You are insolent!"

"The question was put according to custom. It was answered in a way which made it impossible for me to act on my own. The Council would have been the first to condemn me had Dumarest been executed without a hearing. You made the decision as to his fate, not I."

"He is spreading dissension," said Vole. "Instead of being grateful to us for having allowed him to live, he sows the seed of discord." His eyes moved, settled on Althea. "And you are to blame."

An accusation which once would have filled her with trepidation but now she looked at Vole with new eyes. An old man, spiteful in his physical weakness, clinging to power for the sake of pride. An arrogant fool who stormed and threatened but who could be broken like a twig by any man with the courage to defy him. And she had just such a man. One who had taught the hollowness of her previous fears.

"I deny that!"

"What? You dare—"

"To question? Yes. Are you above error? Can you never be wrong?"

"Be silent!" Lelia Logan spoke from where she sat. Her face was ugly with rage. "Are you mad, girl? Have you forgotten who we are? What we are? The destiny of the Terridae lies in our hands. Would you have us forget our duty as you seem to have forgotten yours?"

A blast meant to crush and one which would have done but now Althea saw her as she saw Vole: small, waspish, vicious, reacting to personal fear instead of taking a broad view. As Dumarest had predicted she would act. As he had predicted the reactions of others.

But not of Volodya. He was an unknown quality, sitting calmly behind his mask of detachment; yet his eyes were never still, moving from one to the other, and the hand he had rested on the table was clenched into a fist.

Now he said, "The problem seems to be that Dumarest continues to insist he originated on Earth. Naturally this has made him the object of attention, especially among the young. They are curious and want to learn more. Some even believe that Dumarest was sent to herald the Event."

"Nonsense!"

"Perhaps." Volodya did not look at Vole. "But how can we be certain? The man was barely questioned and never tested."

"For reasons which were explained," snapped Logan. "The Council has no need to justify its actions. Even less to justify its decisions. The man must be silenced!"

The voice of established authority spoke as Dumarest had predicted when, lying in his arms, she had snuggled close to him during the hours of rest. The fear which now she could recognize. How right he had been! Power corrupted and was insidious in its attraction. Back in her chair she leaned back, half-closing her eyes, feeling again the touch of his body, hearing again the whisper of his voice.

"You see it on a thousand worlds and the pattern is always the same. Some begin to issue the orders and find others to help them enforce them. The rest follow like sheep and soon the habit of obedience is instilled. It becomes a conditioned reflex. The voice of authority becomes the voice of God, and those who rule begin to think of themselves as something superior to the rest. A delusion—they are just the same. Only obedience keeps them in power. Remove it and they are helpless."

As Vole would be helpless, as Logan and Gouzh and all who sat on the Council. Althea looked at them from beneath her lowered lids, despising what she saw.

Watching her, Volodya recognized her expression and guessed its cause. Dumarest had been more clever than he'd thought. He'd taken the woman and manipulated her mind as, lost in passion, she had yielded him her body. As even now he and his companion were manipulating the minds of others. Demich? A possibility but the man had always held a wry and cynical attitude toward the Council. A man who took a delight in the breaking of puffed egos; using words as swords to cut inflated pride down to size. Not liked by Vole and the others of his kind; tolerated only because they had no choice.

Would he be ordered to silence him too?

Would he obey such an order?

Volodya looked at his hand, the fist it made, and deliberately opened his fingers. Such a stance was a warning to the observant and he had long learned to reveal nothing of his innermost feelings. To guard the Terridae, to obey the Council, to be efficient at all times—the rules which had governed his life.

Rules sufficient for the small world of Zabul but Dumarest had arrived and with him brought something new. A concept which meant the end of stability as he knew it. A change the Council wanted to resist—and it was becoming obvious why.

Demich summed up the problem. "You talk of silencing a voice which has come among us to herald truth. After that,

what? More murders to silence those who listened to what he
had to say? And even more to silence those who listened to
those who listened? Where will it end?"

"Not the truth!" Logan was adamant. "He lied!"

"And continues to lie!" Vole joined her protest. "He weak-
ens our authority!"

"One man?" Demich shook his head and glanced at Volodya. "I think, Urich, we had better see this monster again."

Dumarest was busy examining Zabul. His guide was a
young man more eager to ask questions than to answer them.
As he led the way down a long corridor he said, "And, at
summer, do the fish rise to the surface to carry people over
the waves?"

"It could happen."

"But then it is never really summer, is it?" Medwin had
barely paused for the answer. "The climate is always warm,
with cooling breezes and stimulating showers which hold sweet
scents. For snow and ice and tall peaks you move to another
part of Earth. As you do to enjoy forests and wide expanses
of soft sand on which to hold games and to manipulate craft
made of wood with winged sails."

"The climates vary, yes." It was a relief to be able to tell
unadorned truth.

"Many climates?"

"From freezing to baking." The conditions to be found on
most worlds but, born and raised in the confines of Zabul,
Medwin found them hard to understand. "The sky changes
too," continued Dumarest. "Sometimes it's blue and then
there could be cloud."

"Blue cloud?"

"White through to a dull gray. And there is snow and hail
as well as rain. The sunsets and dawns are of scarlet and gold,
and, after a rainfall, you can see rainbows arching from horizon to horizon."

"And a silver moon?"

"Yes."

"I'd like to see that," said the young man. "Really see it, I
mean. Land on it so as to observe Earth from space. What
does it look like?" He gave Dumarest no time to answer.
"And the soaring towers of crystal! The Shining Ones! The
places where you can go to make a wish come true!"

Embellishments added by Kusche, who, while chafing at the prison Dumarest had closed about him, worked with his undeniable skill. Selling a glittering illusion of Earth and bolstering the conviction that the Event was close at hand.

"What is this place?" Dumarest paused to look at massive doors. "The power source?"

"No, the Archives." Medwin gestured toward the far end of another passage which ran from a nearby junction. "The power generators are down there. Some of them—we have dispersed all essential units."

An obvious precaution; Dumarest had learned enough to respect those who had fabricated the basic heart of Zabul.

No world could be safe for the Terridae. Always there would be the danger of storm and quake, or fire and rebellion, of cosmic hazard and man-made destruction. Only on a small world which they could keep free of all other forms of life and all other warring threats could they feel safe. Space was the natural haven.

Zabul had been built on a nub of rock which had been gouged out to receive machines to generate power and heat, water and air. One covered with a layer of obsolete vessels, their hulls strengthened, communicating passages established, chambers widened and sealed against the void. A nucleus which had grown with later additions until now it reflected light from a thousand points and spires and curved surfaces. A bizarre fabrication which drifted in a void.

Dumarest looked again at the massive doors. The Archives. The sacred repository of knowledge—and where he would find the location of Earth if it was known. And it had to be known. Had to be!

"Earl?" Medwin was waiting, his face puckered in a frown. "Something wrong?"

"No." Dumarest drew in his breath, conscious of the thudding beat of his heart. To be so near! To have the answer almost in his hand! Yet, for now, he still had to be patient. "Can anyone consult the Archives?"

"Only with Council permission. Did you want to see the reclamation plant?"

A mass of pipes and tubes and the soft hum of leashed power as machines took waste and recycled it into usable material. After that came the chemical refinery, the workshops, the mills. Glass walls protected the crèche. The hydro-ponic gardens were a riot of controlled vegetation.

At one end a lamp flashed in irregular pulses and Medwin went to talk into a phone. When he returned he said, "A summons from the Council, Earl. They want to see you." Laughing, he added, "I guess they want you to tell them about Earth."

He'd guessed wrong and Dumarest knew it as soon as he entered the chamber. The faces of those who sat at the table were too hard, too cold, the eyes too watchful. They stripped and assessed him as he crossed the floor to take the desig-nated chair. A calculated move; standing he would have dominated the assembly. A fact Althea noted as she glanced toward him, noting the set of his mouth, the thin ridge of muscle at his jaw. The face of a man who scented danger and had prepared himself to fight.

Gouzh broke the silence. "You were offered a choice," he said. "One we understood you had accepted." He glanced at Althea. "To work with us and to become one of us." He paused as if waiting for a comment. When none came he added, "It seems we were mistaken."

Dumarest remained silent.

"You have caused trouble," snapped Vole. "Spread rumor and lies. Created unrest and thrown our authority into ques-tion."

"You have proof of this?"

"Proof?" Logan bared her teeth in anger. "We are the Council of Zabul! Dare you say we lie?"

"I am saying you should be prepared to substantiate your charges," said Dumarest evenly. "Rumor and lies, you say, but refuse to be specific. What have I said or done you do not hold to be true?"

"You claim to be from Earth!"

"A backward planet," he reminded her. "One seeking greatness by the local use of a hallowed name. Your own words. As to the rest of the charge, what can I say? If to an-swer questions is to create unrest then I am guilty. But how else should I have acted toward my colleagues? I understood that I was to be one of you and a part of your society. That was the choice I was given."

Demich said, "That is true."

"Be silent!"

"Now wait a moment, Lelia Logan!" The mask had gone, the air of amused and cynical detachment, and the real man blazed with a cold anger. "I am of the Council and your equal. An Elder of Zabul. Am I to grovel at your feet?"

"You—" She broke off, fighting to master her anger. "We are faced with a threat to our society. It is hardly the time to argue on points of protocol."

"I disagree." Gouzh, jealous of his pride, was quick to Demich's defense. "You demand respect but seem unwilling to give it. An apology is in order."

"That will not be necessary," said Dumarest. "I appreciate the sentiment but I did not take offense at the charges." He added blandly, "Mistakes are common among the old."

A clever man, thought Volodya in the shocked silence. One who knew how to exploit a weakness and how to seize an opportunity. He looked at Dumarest with new respect, knowing there had been no mistake, that his assumption had been made with calculated intent. To the casual he had been insolent, to the more discerning he had thrown oil on troubled waters, to those who could see below the surface he had illustrated the unfitness of some of the Council to rule.

One Logan compounded as she spluttered in her rage.

"How dare you! Your defiance goes too far! You will be punished. . . . Guards!"

She screamed the summons and looked at Volodya as men failed to jump at her bidding. For she was old, contaminated with dreams of grandeur while locked in her casket, carrying vestiges of a false greatness into the Council chamber. She and how many others?

"Volodya! Do your duty!"

Vole for one, and Gouzh? He sat, frowning, blinking as if doubting what he saw. Demich was relaxed, sitting back with a faint smile. Rhion looked puzzled. The others, Tilsey, Cade, Kern, sat and said nothing, content to let others make the decisions.

"Volodya!"

He rose, knowing that the impasse had to be broken. He would take Dumarest to a safe place, then return and say what needed to be stated. Changes would be made—Logan for one must relinquish her place.

To Dumarest he said, "Come with me. You will not be harmed, that I promise, but you can accomplish nothing more by staying." He added, "Please do not make me use force."

A man who meant what he said—but how long would he remain in power? And even if he were to ride the storm and reach greater heights, how to ensure he would not weaken to the demands of expediency? Dumarest glanced at the Council, at Althea, who looked at him with pleading eyes. To fight? To run? To yield?

Questions negated by a sudden flood of intense, ruby light.

It filled the chamber, to fade, to return in a crimson haze, to fade and return again. A pulse which could be only one thing.

"Alarm!" Volodya ran to a wall and slammed the palm of his hand on a plate. "Volodya here!" he snapped. "Report!"

The ruby pulse died and a man's voice replaced it in the air. "An unscheduled vessel is approaching Zabul. No recognition signals have been received. Your orders?"

"Yellow alert. Transmit the scene."

A moment and a picture blossomed in the chamber. An expanse of stars transmitted from an external scanner and forming a hologram projection.

"The vessel was spotted in the eighth decant." An arrow blossomed to point to a spot of darkness. "Its present position is here." The arrow moved, faded and where it had pointed showed a faint blue nimbus. The enveloping field of an Erhaft drive. It grew brighter as they watched.

Rhion said, "Renew attempts to contact. It could be a stray vessel unaware of our presence. Warn them of impending collision." He waited. "Well?"

"Message sent but no response."

"Try again."

"Result negative." The voice of the technician held strain.

"Flight path?" Volodya snapped the question. "Is it on a collision course?"

"Yes."

"Sound red alert! No! Wait!" In the projection the blue nimbus had flared to die, to wink out. "Check present position in relation to Zabul."

"Ship has moved into the seventh decant. Still on direct heading."

"Velocity?"

"One third of original and falling." A pause, then, "Contact established."

"An accident." Cade gusted his relief. "Some trader who plotted a bad flight pattern and has just realized it."

Dumarest said, "Are you equipped with warning beacons?"

"No." Volodya glanced at him then back at the depiction. "We don't advertise our presence," he explained. "Zabul is in a location well away from normal shipping routes and we aren't listed in any almanac. This is a private world and we want to keep it that way."

"The Huag-Chi-Tsacowa? Don't they know where you are?"

"No." Volodya saw Dumarest's frown. "You're thinking of deliveries," he said. "They send sealed cargo containers on given courses and we pick them up in space. The courses vary."

But could be plotted to a common point, given enough data and a sharp enough mind to evaluate it. Dumarest looked at the growing fleck on the screen, knowing what it had to be.

To Althea he said, "Zabul isn't a self-sufficient economy. You receive supplies, luxuries, imports, but produce nothing to sell. How do you manage?"

"We own world-based industries."

"Managed by the Vosburgh Consortium?"

"No." It was information she was reluctant to give or did not know. "The first Elders made the arrangements and they've been continued," she said. "Much was sold in order to build Zabul but enough was kept to maintain it. Why, Earl? Is it important.

For him more than that. He looked at the others assembled in the chamber, all now united in the face of a common threat. Though they had yet to realize its strength, it was easy to predict how they would react. For them Zabul and the Terridae would come first. They would have no hesitation in handing him over.

The voice of the technician accompanied the blue haze, which, now returned and brighter than before, drifted close.

"The vessel is the *Saito* and belongs to the Cyclan. It carries Cyber Lim who requests permission to land."

Chapter Twelve

He was tall and thin, his robe like flame, a scarlet envelope masking the gaunt lines of a body devoid of fat and unessential tissue. He kept himself at the height of metabolic efficiency by deliberate privation. The skull was smooth, hairless, the cheeks sunken, the eyes burning pits of intelligence beneath thrusting brows. The man had dedicated his life to the pursuit of logic and reason, had lost the capacity of emotion and had willingly become a living robot of flesh and blood.

Automatically he had been given the high place at the table and now, as he sat, light reflected from the sigil blazoned on the breast of his robe. The sigil was the Seal of the Cyclan and enriched the scarlet as, somehow, it diminished the man. A calculated effect: the organization was everything, those who served it merely cogs in the vast machine. Yet, even so, Lim was impressive.

"My apologies for having intruded on your privacy," he began. "And my congratulations at having hidden your world so well. I find it a place of intense interest and would appreciate the opportunity of a closer examination."

"Perhaps that could be arranged," said Logan.

"You are kind, my lady." The burning eyes held her own for a moment before moving on. A brief glance which had told Lim all he needed to know. She was vain, proud, afraid, eager to please one who could bolster her position. The product of emotional disorder which cursed all who did not wear the scarlet robe. "It may be that I could be of help."

"We have no need of help." Volodya was curt. "What is your business with us?"

"I want the man Dumarest." He heard the sharp intake of the woman's breath, a grunt, saw the looks passed one to the other and felt the glow of mental achievement, which was the only pleasure he could know. The prediction that Dumarest would be on Zabul had been high, but even so nothing was certain. "He is here?"

Volodya dodged the question. "Why do you want him?"

"For reasons which do not concern you."

"I think they do."

"I suggest that what you think need not be of importance." Lim turned to the others, to Logan and Vole. The smooth, even modulation of his voice did not change but they were aware of a subtle menace. "Supplies are delivered to you by the Huag-Chi-Tsacowa and you have arranged a novel form of handling. If, however, the carriers were to be persuaded to end their contract with you, the situation could be difficult." He continued without waiting for comment. "The lands to the south of the Great Water on Legault are devoted to the growing of piksen. The pods are of high medicinal value, yet their active ingredient could be synthesized in factories closer to their market. If that were done the income from the crop would fall drastically. The prediction that within three seasons the land would be more a liability than an asset is of eighty-nine percent probability."

Logan swallowed. The lands he spoke of were a source of Zabul's income.

"There are also mines on Bruzac," said Lim. "They need water which is purchased from the Willcox-Linden Company. They depend on a dam. If that dam should be breached the mines would be bereft of water and would cease production. The prediction of total ruin is ninety-nine percent."

So close to certainty as to make no difference and the message was plain. Cooperate or suffer the consequences and he had made it plain what they would be.

"Threats," said Demich. "I had thought better of the Cy-clan."

"We do not threaten," corrected Lim. "We do not take sides or give advice. For those who hire the service of the Cy-clan we merely predict the logical outcome of events. Each action must have a reaction and to extrapolate the most probable sequence of events is the talent of every cyber. Have I threatened? I merely pointed out the logical outcome of certain actions if those actions should be taken. I could, with equal ease, illustrate the steps it would be wise to take to avoid those consequences."

"Which are?"

Lim glanced at Logan. "As yet you have not hired my services, my lady."

"But if we should? Can't you give us a clue?"

"If you apply and are accepted then a cyber will give you the use of his skill. If you do not then no help can be obtained. Of course," he added, "there is no obligation on you to make use of the predictions once they are given."

But they would be used, for to ignore them was to invite disaster and, once used, they would be impossible to reject. To have the knowledge of what would happen if certain actions were taken. To foresee difficulties. To be able to predict the future—a lure hard to withstand and, dazzled by the possibilities, few reckoned the price.

To hire the services of the Cyclan was to yield power to the organization. A fact rarely displayed and mostly unsuspected but which worked to meld each gained world into a part of the Great Plan. The aim and object of the Cyclan: to achieve total domination over all the galaxy.

Against that design Zabul was of no importance. An artificial world housing those lost in emotional dreams, it could contribute nothing of advantage. It held no financial influence, controlled no affiliated planets, was associated with no strong allies. A world alone that could be treated with disdain.

But Lim knew better than to voice the obvious. Devoid of pride himself, yet he could appreciate how the emotional poison affected others. Knew, also, how to manipulate those prone to longings of grandeur.

"One man," he said. "A single individual against the welfare of your world. Have the Terridae worked so hard and waited so long for one man to bring them ruin?" He paused, waiting for the words to register. Then added the other half of the idea. "The Cyclan is generous to those aiding its servants. Help me and, in turn, you will be helped."

Volodya said, "The question is academic. We neither want

nor need help from the Cyclan. I'm afraid, Cyber Lim, you have had a wasted journey."

"Are you saying that Dumarest is not here?"

"No," snapped Logan. "He is not saying that." She glared at Volodya. "He merely forgets who are the Elders of Zabul."

"The Council must decide," rumbled Vole. "These are matters to think about."

But not for long and Lim knew what the answer would be. Dumarest was a stranger but obviously had sown discord. The woman wanted to be rid of him and she had support. Against it Volodya could do little. Soon now, Dumarest would be in his hands.

Luck, he thought. The unpredictable workings of chance, which could work both ways. Now it was running for him and his future would be assured. A higher sphere of influence would place him closer to the summit of the Cyclan hierarchy. A step to the ultimate position in which he could be elected Cyber Prime. It was possible; proven merit was always rewarded but at the least he would have earned the right to join the massed brains which formed Central Intelligence. To rest among them, divorced from weak and hampering flesh, to spend endless millennia in the gestalt of freed intelligences.

If nothing else, the capture of Dumarest would give him that.

The place had an acrid smell: the stench of acids and chemicals and metallic substances together with the residue of vaporized alkaloids. Dumarest finished closing the box which lay before him on a bench and carefully wiped his hands. They quivered a little and his face was sticky with sweat. Before continuing he washed at a sink, letting water gush over his head and the nape of his neck. The muscles above his shoulders were knotted with strain.

"Earl?" Nubar Kusche called from outside the door as Dumarest made the final adjustment. "Can I come in?"

"A moment." Dumarest wiped the top of the bench, threw the swabs into a disposal bin, and checked the seals of the box. "Right!"

Kusche was suspicious, his eyes searching the room, halting as they rested on the box. "You crazy bastard!"

"Who told you?"

"No one, but I heard you'd asked to be provided with a test lab and some assorted chemicals. Medwin mentioned a couple and said something about a switch." He gestured at the box. "Is that it?"

Dumarest nodded.

"How the hell did you know how to make a bomb?" Kusche didn't wait for an answer. "You've been a miner, right? And a mercenary? Maybe an engineer? All get to know something about explosives. Man, you're crazy! Why not just wait it out? The youngsters are with you and will stand firm. Why risk your neck?"

"To save it," said Dumarest. "And it's yours, too, remember?"

"You don't have to remind me." Kusche scowled. "One way or the other my neck's on the block. But why not see what happens? The Council may refuse to let you go."

A chance Dumarest had assessed and one he couldn't rely on. To hand him over to the Cyclan would be good policy from the point of those who held power. Given more time he might have been able to command greater support but Lim had arrived too soon.

And he could guess at the threats the cyber would make.

He reached for the bomb and looked at Kusche as the man picked it up.

"You made it, Earl," he said. "At least I can carry it. Place it too if you tell me where."

"There's only one place."

"On the Cyclan ship?" Kusche nodded as if he'd already thought it out and was pleased at Dumarest's verifying his conclusion. "Now I know you're crazy. It's veered off, didn't you know?"

"I've been busy."

"Damned busy." Kusche hefted the box. "This thing's big enough to blow the top off a mountain and I'll bet every grain cost a gallon of sweat. Triggered?"

"Time and radio impulse."

"Safety?"

Dumarest said dryly, "I didn't intend committing suicide. It's safe until primed."

"This thing?" Kusche looked at a small, red knob. "Pull it and she's ready, is that it?"

"Why the questions?"

"I want to know what to do." Kusche touched the back. "Limpet-layer. Strip and apply. You make that too?"

"No." Dumarest headed toward the door. "It came from stock. And why do you want to know what to do?"

"We're partners, Earl. You made it and I'll fix it." Kusche was serious. He fell into step beside Dumarest as he headed down the outside passage. "Call it pride, if you like, but I've ridden on your back long enough. It's time I paid my way."

Dumarest said, "Have you worn a suit? Had experience in the void?"

"Have you?"

"I've done undersea work and held a job on a salvage team. If you want to help, give me a hand suiting up and stand by the lock."

It was at the summit of a pinnacle reached through triple doors and guarded by a combination lock. One Dumarest opened with the information given him by Althea. Beyond lay a chamber walled in screens which gave the impression they were of glass. Depicted in them, space was empty but for stars and a single, drifting mote.

"The ship," said Kusche. "Once the bomb is fixed we call the tune. Go home or go to hell! Now where's that suit?"

It rested in its slot and Dumarest checked it before donning the plastic envelope and sealing the helmet. Air whispered in his ears as he stepped into the orifice of the air lock, Kusche handing over the bomb before rotating the compartment into space. A step and Dumarest was on the slope of the pinnacle, held by the gravity zone of Zabul. Flexing his knees, he sprang upward and was suddenly spinning in free fall as he broke the attraction. A moment later he had corrected the spin to hang drifting while he searched for his target.

It hung against the background of burning stars more majestic now in their naked splendor. A tiny ovoid which occluded the brightness, and Dumarest moved toward it with the aid of the power-jets built into his suit. Against the bulk of Zabul he would be invisible to casual observation and he was moving to slowly to activate the vessel's alarms.

But if the vessel should move while he was within the zone of the Erhaft field he would die.

A real danger; ships moved at the dictates of computer directives and the system could have been set to maintain a constant distance from Zabul, to follow a random flight path as a security precaution, or even to twitch away from any object, no matter how small or slow-moving, heading toward it.

Or Lim, tired of waiting, could have decided to take more positive action.

Dumarest altered his course a little, aiming to reach the ship toward the rear section housing the drive mechanism. The hull slapped gently against the soles of his boots and he flexed his knees to cushion the impact. The bomb was clumsy in his gloved hands and he turned it, examining the fuse. In the starlight his face took on the savage ferocity of a primitive idol. For a long moment he worked on the device then stripped off the limpet-cover. A push and the mass was firm against the metal of the hull. A jump and he headed back toward Zabul.

Urich Volodya was waiting for him in the lock.

He stood very tall and determined, two of his guards at hand. Young men armed with clubs and guns firing gouts of stunning gas. Short-range weapons but effective in limited areas. Kusche was nowhere to be seen.

"I'm sorry," said Volodya when Dumarest had opened his helmet. "I must ask you to come with me."

"Ask? Have I a choice?"

"No." Volodya sounded regretful. "I could wish things were otherwise but circumstances leave no alternative. Please remove your suit. I must warn you that the guards have orders to restrain you if you are foolish enough to attempt resistance."

Words well chosen—he could resist but never escape.

As Dumarest returned the suit to its slot he said, "I assume that Cyber Lim has persuaded the Council to hand me over."

"That is correct."

"Did you agree with the decision?"

"I am not of the Elders."

"Which isn't answering my question," said Dumarest. "Or perhaps you did answer it after all. And the price? You surely aren't handing me over for nothing?" He turned as if to make a last inspection of the suit, then smiled at Volodya. "You didn't answer. If you sold me cheap you made a mistake. After all, with me goes your hope of ever living to see the Event."

"So you say."

"Why do you think I'm so important to the Cyclan?"
Dumarest left the question hanging as he moved toward the
door. Volodya stepped back, one of the guards following his
example. The other, lingering, went down as Dumarest
stunned him with a blow to the neck.

"You fool! Guard—"

Volodya's voice died as Dumarest jumped through the
doorway and slammed the panel shut behind him. The combination lock spun uselessly beneath his hand. One of the
triple doors opened as the guard came from behind, a writh-
ing cloud of greenish vapor spouting from his gun. It reached
Dumarest as, holding his breath, he flung open the door and
dived through. Hitting the floor he rolled, sucking air, rising
to lunge at the second door. Behind him Volodya snapped his
impatience.

"Wait, you fool! Hit the gas and you'll be affected. Don't
fire again until he is facing you!"

The guard's inexperience won Dumarest time and he put it
to good advantage. The final door yielded and he raced down
a passage, turned at a junction, ran on to turn again and lose
himself in a complex maze. One stranger to him than to the
residents of Zabul but even they would need time to isolate
and corner him.

How to escape?

No—how to survive?

A woman stared at him as he rounded a corner calling after him as she recognized who he was.

"Earl! Wait! I want to ask you what the Shining Ones do
when—"

The question broke off, unfinished, as he ran on.

Ahead he caught the flash of movement and veered down
a nearby corridor, to emerge in a chamber set with arching
beams and windows which gave onto a misty vastness apparently as spacious as the nave of a tremendous cathedral.
Then he readjusted his orientation and knew the vision to be
the product of illusion. The scenes were set behind lensed
windows which expanded visual horizons and provided the
stuff of endless yearnings.

A moment later he had traversed the area, leaving those
enamored with distance hardly aware that he had come and
gone.

More movement and the sharp blast of a horn, then he was heading down a long slope past windows set with wide-eyed faces. A cage which parted its door became an elevator which whisked him down to lower levels. An area of chill and softness in which echoes died and his pursuers could be within touch and still remain unheard. To either side caskets rested like waiting sarcophagi and he checked them as he ran, counting, watching, halting when he saw the one he had been looking for.

Althea's casket, and he reached it, fighting for breath, chest heaving as he lifted the lid and stared at the soft padding inside. A moment in which he fought the temptation to climb inside and close the lid and seal himself in a private heaven. One he knew could only be the short prelude to a lasting hell.

Stooping, he lifted the knife from his boot and thrust it up and under the upper rim of the casket to the right of the opened expanse. It lanced into the padding and stayed there invisible to a casual eye. Closing the lid he ran on.

"Halt!" The voice roared flatly before him. "You cannot escape!"

A fact Dumarest knew but the guard went down as a fist slammed into his stomach and Dumarest snatched his club and gun before racing on. Time won to put distance between himself and the casket. Time to head toward the reclamation plant where more guards were waiting. One lifted his gun and fired and Dumarest felt his senses swim as green vapor wreathed his face and head in a stifling cloud. Through it the guards were indistinguishable blurs that ducked as he lifted his hand and arm to send the gun flying to ring on a metal stanchion.

They ducked again as he ran at them with the club and fired as he staggered, shrouding him in emerald mist, watching as, already unconscious, he sank to sprawl helplessly on the floor.

Chapter Thirteen

———•◆•———

Dumarest woke to find himself lying naked on a narrow cot in a small room with a barred grill for a door. A cell which could not be mistaken for what it was. The cot lay in a corner and he touched the wall at his side, feeling the faint tingle of transmitted vibration. The quiver grew louder as he rested his ear against the metal: words, the sound of movement, the dull impact of masses colliding, but all merged into a susurration which robbed each of individual clarity.

Against it the clang of the opening door rang like bells.

Urich Volodya said, "It is useless to pretend you are unconscious. I know you are awake."

He stood beside the cot, haloed in a nimbus of light, seeming taller because of his position. One not so close as to be careless but close enough to display his confidence. A guard stood at the opened door, armed, alert, and Dumarest guessed others would be outside.

"Are you ill?" Volodya frowned as Dumarest rolled his head, gasping, pretending a weakness he did not feel. "The gas is harmless but you had a heavy dose." And it could affect those with unsuspected allergies in unusual ways. As Dumarest raised himself, slowly and with obvious effort, Volodya called, "A stimulant! Quickly!"

It came in a container of thin plastic material which would not shatter or hold an edge. A precaution Dumarest could appreciate even as he regretted the lost opportunity. Volodya, with death at his throat, could have provided a valuable hostage.

"Drink," he ordered. "Immediately!"

Dumarest obeyed, sipping the pale azure fluid, feeling strength well from his stomach as the drugs gave him chemical energy. As he finished the drink Volodya threw him a robe of pale amber material.

"Wear this."

Rising, Dumarest slipped on the robe. The fabric was thin, moulding itself to his body and reaching barely to mid-thigh. It was held by an adhesive band on the edge. As Volodya stepped toward the door Dumarest sat on the edge of the cot.

"You are to come with me," said Volodya. "To defy me would be futile and childish."

"I'm not defying you," said Dumarest. "But those who gave you your orders."

"The Council—"

"Are dancing to an alien tune. They obey the cyber and you know it. Which means you have become his willing servant. So much for the Guardian of Zabul."

"You have a choice," said Volodya coldly. "You can walk with dignity and pride or you can be dragged struggling every step of the way. Which is it to be?"

A hard man, thought Dumarest, leaning back to rest his shoulders against the wall. One who couldn't be pushed and who justified everything he did. To arrest a prisoner—a matter of obeying an order. To take him where directed—another order to be obeyed. But such a man would never have gained his position if he had been nothing more than an obedient machine. How to stimulate his ambition? His curiosity?

At his back the wall murmured with vibration, sounds rising like rocks in an ocean, a shout, a thudding, the rasp of what could have been metal.

Dumarest said quietly, "I will not make your task harder. You already have enough on your hands as it is."

"You know?" Volodya stared his incredulity. "But you have been unconscious and no one has visited you. How did you know those young fools were demanding your release?"

Kusche's work? A possibility but Dumarest knew the strength and speed of rumor. A technician or a guard who had passed the word and one would have been enough to arouse the predicted reaction. To the young he was their hope of witnessing the Event. Volodya was the instrument of those robbing them of their dream.

And what could he or the Council know of rebellion?

What could these of Zabul?

Lim would ignore them as troublesome vermin. If they defied him he would threaten to destroy their world and would do it without compunction. To rely on popular support was to invite destruction.

Dumarest said, "You are too intelligent to resist advice when your survival is at stake. It is true that one man cannot be set against the value of a world, but do not make the mistake of underestimating the Cyclan. Against a cyber the Council are like ignorant children. He will use and manipulate them all along the line. You must have sensed this."

"So?"

"The Council are wrong and you know it. They are old and clinging to power. They don't want to find Earth—do you?"

Volodya said, stiffly, "We all long for the Event."

"You, Althea, some others. You could name them better than I. And the young, of course. The young are always impatient." Casually Dumarest added, "What are they doing? Demonstrating? Shouting and making a noise? Clogging the passages? Neglecting their duties? What happens if they refuse to obey orders? You need them to maintain the system. What happens if they demand to retire to their caskets?"

He gave Volodya time to ponder the question as, again, he leaned his shoulders against the wall. His initial reaction had been wrong; Zabul had no separate working class. The young of the Terridae maintained the artificial world, not being entitled to a casket unitl they had reached full maturity. Even then custom dictated they use them rarely until advancing years gave them the right to extend their lives to the full.

A nice, neat, well-organized culture but brittle as such cultures always had to be. His arrival had cracked it and now Lim threatened to shatter it with his demands. A fact Volodya recognized.

He said, "What can I do? Cyber Lim has warned he will destroy Zabul unless you are handed over to him. He could be bluffing but I dare not take the chance."

"The Cyclan does not bluff."

"So I gathered. It helps that you understand. For you, as a person, I have only respect. If circumstances were different I would like to be your friend. As it is—" Volodya broke off, shrugging. "Now you must come with me."

"Of course," said Dumarest. "But hadn't we better work out how to get things back to normal first?"

Volodya hesitated, looking at his prisoner. A man almost naked, certainly unarmed, knowing what his fate would be yet sitting with a relaxed ease he found hard to understand. As he found it impossible to know how Dumarest could quell the unrest his arrest had created.

"What can I do?"

"You alone? Nothing." Dumarest was blunt. "You stand for the Council and the power of the Cyclan. They have no reason to trust you. But there are others, Demich, Althea Hesford. Althea," he decided. "We were close and they would know it. They will trust what she has to say. What I will tell her to say. Send for her and let us be alone."

A trick? What could Dumarest do? Volodya hesitated, then, knowing he had no alternative, nodded his agreement.

"I'll give you ten minutes—Lim will be getting impatient. But can you guarantee to restore peace and order?"

"How can I? I'm in no position to guarantee anything." Dumarest hardened his tone. "But one thing is certain— unless I try, Zabul will tear itself apart. Now hurry and get Althea!"

They were taking too long; the prediction he had made as to when Dumarest would be in his hands had turned out to be at fault. An error Lim found unpleasing and he quested for reasons to account for it. Had he underestimated his adversary? Judged the capabilities of the Council too highly? Forgotten some small but signifcant factor which should have been included in his assessment of the situation?

If the last, it was proof of his failing capabilities but, with cold detachment, he examined the possibility. An exercise conducted with the speed and skill of long training and longer experience and the summation was satisfactory. The reason had to lie elsewhere. Dumarest was clever and resourceful but limited by his situation, and his capture was inevitable. Those responsible for taking him, then, were to blame for the delay.

Leaning forward, he touched a communicator and, as it

flashed into life, said, "Contact Zabul and find why the delivery of Dumarest is taking so long."

"Yes, Master."

As always the acolyte was respectful and as always he would be efficient—should he be otherwise then he would have proved himself unfit to don the scarlet robe. A hard apprenticeship and one every cyber had to take.

Lim looked at the papers lying before him: data on a score of problems on the world he had left to pursue Dumarest. Some of them would now have been resolved, while others must have risen, but, while waiting, it would be inefficient to waste time. Quickly he studied the reports, made his assessments, noted the predictions as to the order of probability. The salon was quiet, the ship carried no passengers other than himself and his acolytes, and the crew wore padded shoes.

A soft chime and his communicator flashed for attention. The face of Hulse stared from the screen.

"Master, a report from Zabul. Dumarest has been taken but had to be gassed before capture. He has now recovered consciousness and will be dispatched as soon as arrangements have been made."

"Why the further delay?"

"Shipping sacs have to be prepared. The alternative would be to move the ship and make physical contact with Zabul."

After a moment for assessment Lim said, "No. The possibility of danger is small but there is no point in taking risks without cause."

"The demonstrators are dispersing."

"Even so our presence may excite them to take action to protect Dumarest." And the violence could result in accidental injury to the man concerned. "Full instructions have been given?"

"Yes, Master."

The screen died and Lin made a mental note to recommend Hulse's elevation. The acolyte had showed his ability and demonstrated his efficiency. No wasted words. No repetition of the obvious. If he had arranged for the transfer to be handled correctly he would be ready for the final tests.

Lim checked the last of the papers and set them in their file. Now he had nothing to do but wait and yet not even a moment should be wasted. Dumarest was in custody; soon he would be on his way to the vessel and, once inside, his journeying would be over. Drugged, bound, locked in a cell, he would be helpless to escape. Not even his clothes had been left to him and, almost naked, what could he do?

Rising, the cyber crossed the salon and made his way to his cabin. Here, on the ship, there was no need for an acolyte to stand guard but even so he locked the door before activating the broad band he wore on his left wrist. Mechanisms within the wide bracelet created a zone of electronic privacy which no prying eye or ear could penetrate. Lying on the narrow cot, Lim stared at the ceiling. To wait or to report?

The temptation to wait was strong but even stronger was the experience he knew awaited him. He had cause—it was his duty to report, and the charge of inefficiency could be laid against him if he did not. To wait was to seek personal aggrandizement.

Relaxing, he closed his eyes and concentrated on the Samatchazi formulae. Gradually he lost the power of his senses; had he opened his eyes he would have been blind. Locked in the confines of his skull, his brain ceased to be irritated by external stimuli. It became a thing of pure intellect, its reasoning awareness its only thread of life. Only then did the engrafted Homochon elements become active. Rapport quickly followed.

Lim became vibratingly alive.

He felt himself expand to fill the universe while remaining a part of it. Space was filled with light: sparkles which spun and created abstract designs and yet had a common center. One to which he was drawn, to be engulfed in the tremendous gestalt of minds which rested at the heart of the headquarters of the Cyclan. There, buried beneath miles of rock, set deep in the heart of a lonely planet, the Central Intelligence absorbed his knowledge like a sponge sucking up water. There was no verbal communication, only a mental communion in the form of words: quick, almost instantaneous, organic transmission against which the speed of light was the merest crawl.

The rest was sheer intoxication.

There was always this moment during which the Homochon elements sank back into quiescence and the machinery of the body began to realign itself to the dictates of the mind. Lim drifted in an ebon nothingness, a limbo in which he sensed strange memories and unlived situations—scraps of overflow from other intelligences, the discarded waste of other minds.

A taste of the heaven he hoped to achieve.

Volodya said, "This is it. Go through that door and wait." He hesitated then held out his right hand, palm upward. "If we don't meet again—"

"You did your duty." Dumarest touched the proffered palm with his own. "Have no regrets."

The man had done what he could and more than what he had needed to have done. Dumarest stepped from him toward the door, hearing a shout from down the passage where a small group stood blocked by guards.

"Give the word, Earl, and we won't let you go!"

Medwin? The face was lost as others surged forward and Dumarest sensed the rising hysteria. A moment and they would break through the cordon. A word of encouragement and they would defend him with their lives.

And Zabul would be destroyed.

"Hold it!" Dumarest faced them, both hands upraised. "Everything's under control," he said. "Just relax and stop worrying. I'll be fine. Just break up and get back to work." He added, to give greater reassurance, "I'll be back."

"You promise?"

Medwin again? Dumarest couldn't be certain but he felt the impact of Volodya's eyes.

"You want me to sign it in blood?" Dumarest smiled as he asked the question. "Just break it up now. Trust Volodya."

As he had trusted Althea—had she let him down?

The room was what he had expected: a chamber with a door at the far end, a table in the center now bearing a tray of wine and cakes with matching goblets. Dumarest looked at them, then at the empty chamber. Empty but, he guessed, not unobserved. Someone, somewhere, would be checking his every move and he would be making a fatal mistake to forget it.

The far door, as he'd expected, was locked and he returned to the table to pour himself a little wine and to pick up one of the cakes. He was clumsy and it fell from his hand to land on the floor. Stopping, he picked it up, throwing a quick glance at the underside of the table, feeling relief as he saw a familiar object held by a wad of gekko-plastic at the far end.

His knife—Althea had not let him down.

Dumarest rose and sat at the table, sipping his wine and slowly eating the cake. Casually he lowered his hands beneath the table, found the knife, pulled it free and let his fingers drift over the comforting metal. The blade with its curves, razor-sharp edges, the needle point, the scarred guard, the worn hilt which ended in a pommel held by a narrow line of weld. Holding the hilt in one hand, Dumarest twisted the pommel with the other, a surge of energy carefully masked, and the pommel spun free to expose the hollowed interior of the hilt to his questing fingers.

The two halves of the affinity twin fell into his palm.

He held them beneath his thumb while he replaced the pommel and thrust the knife back against the clinging plastic. It was hard to hide his relief. He had hidden the weapon in the one place Althea would be certain to know, throwing the gun he had snatched from the guard into the reclamation plant as a decoy. That seemed to have worked—Volodya hadn't mentioned the missing knife.

Why was he being left alone so long?

The cyber would be eager to have him safe and he had delayed as long as he could, telling Volodya it would make things easier for Althea to quiet the crowd but in reality to gain her time to recover the knife and plant it beneath the table. To get her to do other things, too, but they were of less importance.

"Earl!" Nubar Kusche entered the room through the door which had been locked. "I heard—man, why do it?"

"I've no choice."

"We could fight—no." Kusche scowled, deep lines marring the round plumpness of his face, the space between his eyes. "They'd wreck Zabul and you'd still be taken. But there must be something we can do. That bomb?"

"Isn't going to work." Beneath the edge of the table Dumarest fingered the two ampules. Each was tipped with a hollow needle and one was red while the other was green. Colors he couldn't see but the red had a ridged surface while the green was smooth. "But you know that already."

"I know—what the hell are you talking about?"

"I checked the detonator," said Dumarest. "Is that enough?"

"You should have died," said Kusche bitterly. "Gone out in a puff of glory and taken that damned ship with you. As soon as you primed the bomb it should have been over." He frowned, realizing the significance of what he was saying. "You checked," he said slowly. "That means you didn't trust me."

"No."

"But—"

"You put on a good act," said Dumarest. "But as I told you you're an entrepreneur, not a gambler, and following that casket was nothing but a gamble. And you were too vague about having been knocked out with gas while in your bunk—why should the Huag-Chi-Tsacowa have gone to that trouble? They have ethics. They would never have betrayed their client like that."

"The Cyclan—"

"Yes," said Dumarest. "The Cyclan." The green ampule was against his wrist and he pressed, feeling the needle bury itself into his flesh. A tiny spark of pain which told of the dominant half of the affinity twin entering his body to move through it and settle at the base of his cortex. "A chance," he said. "One you took for pay and the prospect of high reward. But if the Cyclan had been on Caval and known I was in that casket it would never have been shipped out."

"You bastard! You smart, cunning bastard!" Kusche paused, fighting his anger. "I could have sold you," he said. "I would have sold you but you took care of that. The Cyclan will never believe I don't know the secret and they'll kill me for a reason I'll never know. So you have to die, you can see that, can't you? The bomb would have done it clean but there are other ways. No!" He stepped back, his right hand lifting as Dumarest reached for the decanter. "Back off—I mean it! Touch that wine and I'll burn you! I know how damned fast you are!"

Dumarest halted the movement of his hand, lifted the other to scratch idly at his scalp—thrusting the red ampule deep into his hair. How to reach Kusche without inviting death from the laser in his hand?

Dumarest looked at it, small but lethal at short range, a sleeve-gun favored by gamblers and women of a certain kind.

But Kusche had owned no such weapon. Where had he got it?

"Does it matter?" The man shrugged when Dumarest asked. "Zabul is a world full of odd things. Now stand up. Up, damn you! Step from that table! Move!"

He made the mistake of gesturing with the weapon and Dumarest snatched his chance. The wine spilled in a golden stream from the decanter as it spun whirling through the air. A missile Kusche dodged, firing as he sprang to one side, the sear of the laser leaving a scorched patch on a wall. He fired again as a goblet smashed against his forehead, small shards creating minor lacerations. A third time as, ducking, Dumarest snatched at his arm.

It was like grabbing a rod of steel.

The plumpness held muscle, as he had guessed, and Kusche was fighting for his life. Dumarest had no chance to snatch the red ampule from his hair, to use it, to take over Kusche as he'd intended. He ducked again as fingers stabbed at his eyes, struck back in turn, twisted to avoid the knee which smashed upward toward his groin, feeling the impact against his thigh.

"Bastard!" Kusche had forgotten the laser in his anger. "You dirty bastard!"

Again his knee stabbed upward, this time missing completely. Dumarest turned, caught Kusche by the arm, slammed his stiffened palm against the bicep and heard the dull thud as the laser hit the floor. Releasing the arm, he jammed his palm up beneath the other man's chin, felt the jar and shock of a returned blow, and weaved to avoid another.

As the fist passed above his shoulder Dumarest moved in, smashed aside the defense and sank his fingers into Kusche's throat. For a moment they strained face to face, Kusche stiffening his neck and tensing the muscles as his hands rose to tear free the clamping fingers, Dumarest searching for the carotids so as to apply the pressure which would render the other man unconscious.

"No!" Kusche's eyes matched the plea of his voice. "Earl—no!"

He stiffened, then suddenly went limp, his glazed eyes rolling up, mouth curved in the empty grin which was the rictus of death. From his side rose a thread of smoke accompanied by the stench of burned tissue. Dumarest released him and, as he fell, turned to face the door at the end of the chamber and the woman standing before it.

"Well, Earl," said Carina Davaranch, "it seems we meet again."

Chapter Fourteen

———••◆••———

She was as he remembered with the neat helmet of golden hair set close to the rounded skull, the thick brows framing the eyes of vivid blue. A woman who could have been a man with the strong bones of her face, the firm line of her jaw. Her face was now marred by a purple bruise which blotched a cheek and temple.

"Stand away from that filth." The laser in her hand jerked to emphasize the command, fired as he obeyed. Beside the body of Kusche the weapon he had used flared to molten ruin.

"Yours?"

"I had two." She reached for a chair and sat down, her face ghastly beneath the bruise. "The fool never thought of that. He struck me down and found what he wanted and hurried to do what he thought had to be done. I heard him but it took time to recover. Are you hurt?"

"No." Dumarest stepped toward her. "But you are. Let me get you something for that bruise."

"It can wait." The laser in her hand moved only a fraction but it was enough. "Please don't make me use this, Earl. I won't kill you but I'll ruin your knees and elbows if I have to. Believe me, I can do it."

"And after?"

"There are two acolytes waiting outside to carry you to the ship."

Dumarest said nothing, looking at the woman, studying what he saw. She had changed in a way so subtle that he

141

hardly noticed it, then, as he looked, little things became
clear. The clothing helped; she wore masculine-type pants
and boots with a tunic fastened in the same manner as his
robe. The face, too, had changed, losing some of its feminine
softness, so that ever more than before she resembled a delicately fashioned boy.

"Men," she said. "The ship holds only men."

"So?"

"It's catching." She closed her eyes for a moment then
opened them with a start as if she had expected him to have
moved. She relaxed a little when she found he hadn't. "You
don't understand, do you? No more than you understand
what it is to be born a woman in a male-oriented society. For
the boys everything. For the girls nothing. They are just the
bearers of new life, breeders to replenish the race, drudges,
chattels, beasts to be used! My father was a fool and a
vicious one at that. The least he could have done for me was
to see I was born a male. For that alone I hated him."

"And killed him?"

"No, that pleasure was denied me. Do I shock you?"

Dumarest shook his head and reached for the other chair
and sat with the table between them.

"Keep your hands in full view, Earl. Just in case." Her
tone and laser made her meaning clear. "As I said, my father
was a fool. He failed to realize that intelligence is always accompanied by imagination and there is more than one path
to any objective."

"The Cyclan?"

"You guessed." Her shrug did no more than stir her shoulders. "A matter of injections and glandular adjustment together with selective manipulation of certain tissues. They
made me androgynous. In time I will become a true hermaph-
rodite. The best of both worlds," she added bitterly. "While
belonging to none."

A victim of another's ambition, now changed, warped,
twisted. But the fault had always been present: the curse
which made it impossible for her ever to know true happiness
or contentment. How soon had she known? When had she
first tried to run and hide herself among the stars? After the
fertility rite beneath a scarlet moon?

A guess but a good one and Dumarest watched as, again,
her eyes closed to snap open with the same start. A creature

in fear, two tense and too much on edge to be trusted. A false move and she would fire blasts which would leave him a cripple. Yet to leave it too long would be to leave it too late.

"The plan," he said. "Yours?"

"A simple problem—how to find a needle in a haystack. One which moves in a random pattern. That's what the Zaragoza Cluster is, Earl. A haystack, and you were the needle. So I provided the magnet."

"Caval?"

"Yes. A thousand paintings were produced and spread among a hundred worlds to be hung in agents' offices near fields where they would be seen. I went to planets where the probability of your being present was highest. Shard was the third and I was lucky. The boy was set as bait and his companions should have taken you. They failed but it didn't matter—we had made contact. Even when you killed Ca Lee it didn't matter—the painting remained as bait. The only problem was that you moved too fast. That and the accidental burn-damage of a generator which made Cyber Lim arrive on Caval after you had gone."

"With Kusche in attendance."

"A precaution, and the fool was too greedy to recognize his potential danger. Too stupid to spot the flaw in his story which made you suspicious. The Cyclan contacted the Huag-Chi-Tsacowa and made sure he was included in the transfer. By the time you discovered the detector it was too late—we had located Zabul."

And now Kusche was dead. Dumarest looked at him where he lay, mouth open as if smiling at some secret jest, eyes blank, a pool of blood now providing a scarlet mirror at his side.

"I tried, Earl," said Carina as if in justification. "I begged you to stay at the Hurich Complex so as to give Lim time to arrive. I wanted you to stay with me in town, but then you said you were leaving and, well, there was nothing else to do." She frowned as if puzzled. "Who would have guessed you would have had such luck?"

The chance of seeing a reflection in the mirror of a window. Of dodging the searching guards. Of picking the one warehouse to hide in which held the casket for shipping. Of the Huag-Chi-Tsacowa insisting on delivering it. And the greatest luck of all—to have found the Terridae.

She almost seemed to be reading his thoughts. "Luck, Earl, but for you it's over. From now on it's my turn. The treatment finished and I'll be what I want. No more veering from one polarity to another. The way of the universe," she added. "Of scum like Kusche. Your loss my gain—well, that's the way it goes."

He noticed the gesture of her hand toward her bruised face and guessed at her pain. Kusche had not been gentle and the bone could have been fractured: small cracks in temple and cheek.

He said, "Remember back on Shard when you dressed my scalp? Let me return the favor. At least let me get you something to ease the pain."

"Shard," she said. "For a moment there I was happy. Maybe had I met a man like you earlier I could have accepted being a woman." Her tone took on a new bitterness. "Too late, Earl. The story of my life. Everything's always come too damned late." Her voice rose as someone tapped on the door through which Dumarest had entered. "What is it?"

"The sacs, my lady. Everything is now in readiness."

"Coming!" She looked at Dumarest. "Cattaneo," she explained. "One of Lim's acolytes. A robot like the rest of them. I told you it was catching."

"Does he have a friend?"

"I doubt it. But he does have a companion. A creature like himself. Earl! Your hand!"

He had lifted it casually toward his scalp, and he froze the motion, looking at her with a frown.

"My head itches. Mustn't I scratch it?" His tone sharpened with simulated anger. "To hell with this! If we're going, let's go!"

He rose without warning, catching the edge of the table on his knees, lifting it to jar against her hand which held the laser. A movement continued as the weapon swung upward, the weight of the furniture tipping to strike across her torso, to throw her backwards off her chair.

Dumarest followed the table, feeling the sear of the laser as its beam brushed his cheek. Then he was close, hand moving, the red ampule it held driving into the soft flesh of her throat.

And, suddenly, he changed.

"My lady!" The acolyte was no longer young, a man set in his ways, one who would never don the scarlet robe of a cyber but a dedicated servant nonetheless. He entered the room, attracted by the noise, to stand for a moment looking at the mess. Then he stooped, lifting Dumarest by the arms, setting him upright on his feet. "Are you hurt, my lady?"

The pain of the bruise on his cheek and temple, the ache of ribs—the impact of the table had not been gentle. And a sting in the throat from the ampule buried in the flesh. Dumarest lifted his hand to it, tore it free as he shook his head.

"No. I'll be all right." He looked at the man. Cattaneo? A high probability but it was best to avoid names. "Get a sac and prepare Dumarest for travel." He gestured at the body in the pale amber robe lying slumped on the floor.

"Is he—"

"No. He's unharmed but I had to drug him." Dumarest displayed the red ampule. "The other is dead but forget him. Those of Zabul can clear up the mess. Hurry, now, your master will be waiting!"

Dumarest sagged as the acolyte ran to do his bidding, fighting a sudden nausea born of the shock of transition. There had been no time to adjust, none to master the workings of the body which was now his host. Now he straightened, looking at his hands—the fine, delicately strong hands of an artist. The arms covered with the fabric of the tunic, the legs, the torso with its unaccustomed contours. Carina's body now a vehicle in which he rode by the magic of the affinity twin.

Used it and dominated it so that it had become his own. He saw through Carina's eyes, felt with her hands and nerves, walked on her legs and spoke with her voice. The affinity twin had given him total slave-control. With it in their possession the Cyclan would be able to control every person of power and privilege. Offer a bribe no dotard could reject, no crone refuse. To be young again! To own a fresh, virile body.

The secret Kusche hadn't known.

As the acolyte returned with a companion to lift the pale-robed body into a sac Dumarest drew a shuddering breath. His own body was quiescent, operating on its autonomic nervous system, waiting for his conscious ego to regain mastery.

But the link he had established could only be broken by death.

"I'm sorry," he said inwardly. "I had no other choice. You'd killed Kusche and left me no option."

Could she hear? Understand? Or had her own conscious awareness been totally swamped by the invading molecular unit and driven into some formless limbo? But, if not, was she now cringed in some dark corner of her mind wailing in endless terror?

"My lady." The first acolyte looked up from the sac. "We are ready."

"Then let's waste no more time. Go before me. Head directly toward the lock."

Walking ahead, they would notice nothing if he should stagger or act in any unusual way. Burdened with the weight of his body now sealed in the air-tight membrane, they would have little chance of spotting or questioning any activity around them.

In the corridor leading to the lock Dumarest paused to look at Volodya standing attended by a pair of guards. Althea, standing further down the passage, stared at Dumarest with hostile eyes.

"You've hurt him!"

"No. He's drugged, nothing more."

"Must you take him?"

"Surely he explained all that?" Dumarest kept his voice as level as his eyes. Althea seemed to have grown taller than he remembered; the illusion was because of his own new viewpoint. Carina's height was less than his own. He said, "You spoke together, I understand. A lover's parting? Never mind, my dear, there will be others ready to fill your arms."

"You bitch!"

"But a winning one. Dumarest is mine now. Think of what he told you—you'll have nothing else."

He moved on, following the acolytes as they passed into the large area of a loading port. Here an entire vessel could be sealed from the void but other, smaller locks gave passage to items of lesser bulk. Before one lay the crumpled envelopes of three sacs. Zabul technicians stood ready to operate the controls.

"My lady?" One of the acolytes looked at Dumarest. "Are you ready to be placed in a sac?"

"You go first." A mistake and Dumarest corrected it. "No. One of you, then myself, the last to see us passed through the lock then to follow."

A jumble of litter rested beside and around the area: bales, cartons, cases, a heap of what looked like rope but which was a mass of vine from the hydroponic gardens. Men heaved at it, some of them familiar to Dumarest. Close to the vine lay open containers of seed as fine as sand. As Dumarest walked toward the portal a man yelled a warning from somewhere behind.

"Alarm! A plate's cracked!"

The shout was drowned in the blare of a klaxon. As it fell silent a wind sprang to life to roar over the area, catching up assorted fragments and swirling them into a blizzard-like hail. The mass of vine heaved, fine seed pluming upward from the containers to grit eyes and fill nostrils with a stinging odor. For a moment all was wild confusion, then the wind died and the debris settled as the emergency systems came into operation.

"My lady?" The elder of the acolytes was anxious. "Into the sac, my lady. Hurry!"

They drifted from Zabul like elongated bubbles, the membranes puffed from internal air pressure, reflected starlight giving them the appearance of pearls. Those ahead shifted a little as Dumarest watched: small jets blasting vapor into the void and giving a measure of directional control. Would Carina have known how to operate a sac? Dumarest recalled how he had been sealed and evicted and decided that she had no need of instruction. It was safe to manipulate his own controls and draw closer to the others. One of the acolytes turned to face him and gestured ahead. A clear indication to move into the van. Dumarest obeyed, seeing the figures behind the protective transparency, the starlight giving them a peculiar, blurred quality as if seen through misted glass.

A suited figure caught the sac as Dumarest guided it into the open hold of the vessel. The acolyte set it firmly on the deck, then went to help the others. Within seconds after their arrival the ports closed and, as the taut membrane of his sac began to soften beneath external pressure, Dumarest tore at the fastenings. He climbed free before the acolytes, halting the suited figure as he stooped over the sac holding the figure in the amber robe.

"Leave him. Dumarest is safe enough as he is."

"My lady—"

"I am a doctor," snapped Dumarest. "The man had to be drugged. Moving him now will do no good and could lead to later complications. Where is your master?"

Locked in his cabin and in the final stages of rapport. He came to join Dumarest in the salon and stood for a moment looking at the table, the wine it held. A concession to the woman; no servant of the Cyclan had any use for intoxicants.

"You are not drinking."

"No." Carina, unlike Kusche, had not leaned on the comfort of alcohol. "I had thought you would greet us."

"I was otherwise engaged." Lost in a mental paradise which had lasted longer than he had anticipated, as the transfer had happened sooner than predicted. "Dumarest is in the cabin prepared for him?"

"Not as yet."

"But still sealed in his sac?"

"I explained that." Dumarest turned to stare up at the cyber. "Nothing can be gained by moving him while he is still under the influence of drugs. He was in a highly emotional state when faced with the inevitable."

"So you drugged him?"

"I had no choice." Dumarest coughed and tasted blood. Wiping his lips he displayed the carmine smear. "He attacked me, broke a rib; given time he would have broken my neck."

Lim nodded; he had already received the report from Cattaneo. Of how the woman was down, the upturned table beside her, Dumarest sprawled to one side. And of the man lying dead.

Had Kusche allied himself with Dumarest at the end? A possibility which he considered and one backed by the bruise on the woman's face, her obvious internal injuries, Kusche's death. Details now of small importance.

Dumarest said, "When do we leave?"

"You are in a hurry?"

"To gain my reward, yes. I didn't do all this for fun."

"You will receive all you have earned," said Lim evenly. "The Cyclan always keeps its word." The truth—but there was more than one way to keep a bargain. "Hulse!" As the acolyte entered the salon Lim gestured at Dumarest. "Search her."

An examination which he accepted without argument. The touch of the acolyte was deft but thorough. The cyber looked at the small laser Hulse placed on the table close to the wine.

"You had another."

"Ruined. I left it where it lay." Dumarest added, "There was no need of the search. I would have handed it over had you asked."

"Of course. Where did you keep the drug?"

"The one I gave Dumarest? Here, beneath the edge of my tunic." Dumarest gestured with his hand. "I always carry it as a precaution. Some men refuse to take no for an answer."

A logical explanation and Lim seemed to be satisfied. Dumarest coughed again and swallowed a warm, salty wetness. One rib broken, maybe two, and a jagged fragment must have lacerated a lung. Movement would accelerate the slow bleeding but his nerves screamed for action. How long would the cyber take to make up his mind?

"You seem unwell," said Lim. "It would be wise to retire to your cabin. I shall send you medical assistance."

An order it would be stupid to disobey. But which was his cabin?

Dumarest rose and fought a sudden giddiness. Reaching for the wine he said, "You are gracious, but first a toast. I think the moment calls for it." The wine gurgled as he poured and he remembered how Carina had acted when they had shared a meal in the Durand on distant Shard. Lifting the glass he faced the cyber with a smile. "To success, my friend. To the fulfillment of ambition!"

He drank with Lim watching, the cyber making no comment. Setting down the glass, Dumarest walked across the salon to halt at the door. Swaying, he rested one hand on the edge, lifting the other to his bruised face.

"It hurts," he muttered. "And I feel about to faint. Help me, cyber. Help me!"

For a moment he clung to the support, then slowly let his knees buckle to hit the floor, his body following to lie in a helpless sprawl, eyes closed, breathing shallowly. A woman who had fainted and who would need to be carried to her cabin.

Dumarest heard the soft rustle of the cyber's robe, felt the muffled vibration of his footsteps as he came close. The fingers which touched his face were like thin, dry twigs, deft as they lifted an eyelid to expose the rolled-up ball. Fingers moved to probe at the bruise and sent darts of pain lancing through cheek and temple. Dumarest groaned and moved, to lie still again as the delicate touch moved to his throat and the tiny puncture left by the hollow needle of the ampule.

And screamed as a hand smashed down to drive the jagged end of broken bones into his lungs.

Chapter Fifteen

It was a red flood which filled the universe and left him gasping and weak in its savage ferocity. Dumarest had known pain before but this had come with total unexpectedness— and this body was not his own.

He reared, seeing the skull-like visage of the cyber inches above his own. The face turned carmine as Dumarest stained it with the blood he spat from his mouth. As Lim retreated Dumarest struck at the throat, missed, and followed the blow with another with the same result. Fury vented on thin air and effort which tore at his lungs and filled the universe with a fresh tide of pain.

Dumarest rolled to hands and knees, coughed a scarlet flood and fought a mountain of pain to climb to his feet. Staggering, he reached the support of the edge of the door.

From where he stood, well out of reach, Lim said, "Do not attempt anything foolish. I will not hesitate to cripple you should you try."

A machine with a laser in his hand and blood on his face. Carmine which matched the scarlet of his robe and soiled the glitter of the sigil on his breast. One who could feel no anger, know no fear.

Dumarest said, "Why?"

"You made mistakes. Small things which accumulated, but the biggest of all was to take me for a fool. Did you really think I was so inefficient as not to recognize the charade?"

"I don't understand." If the cyber knew the truth there was no point in verifying it. If he was guessing then to be honest

151

was to be stupid. "You hit me." Dumarest lifted a hand to his chest, face registering agony which was real. "I fainted, I think, then you hit me. My reward, cyber? Is that how the Cyclan pays its debts?"

"Sit." Lim gestured to the table, the chair. "Take wine. It contains a stimulant."

One he needed and Dumarest poured a glass full as the cyber left to wash the blood from his face and change into a clean robe. To be dirty was to be inefficient and he saw no immediate urgency demanding his presence. Hulse took his place, the acolyte standing well to one side. Dumarest studied him as he swallowed the wine.

A man a little too cautious and so too highly strung. One who must lose his concentration after a while as the body, keyed for immediate action, rebelled against the strain. Then would be the moment to act if action was possible but Dumarest knew that it was not.

He drank more wine, indifferent as to what it might contain, needing the chemical strength it could give. The stimulant sharpened his senses but did nothing to dull his pain. A calculated effect, he guessed, Lim would not want him to be comfortable.

Dumarest coughed and, dabbing at his lips, looked at the bright scarlet on his hand. Blood which he had spat into Lim's face to blind him. An attack which had failed and he knew again the hurt of inadequacy. He had misjudged, mistimed. His arms had been too short, his reactions too slow. The body he wore was alien in more ways than one. He almost felt hampered by leaden weights. Was this how it felt to be a woman?

Dumarest reached for more wine as Lim returned and tensed, the decanter in his hand. Hulse came to remove it at the cyber's signal, moving in close enough for his skull to be smashed, but Dumarest doubted his ability to hit hard and clean. In any case to kill the acolyte would serve no purpose. He released the decanter and watched as it was removed together with the glass. Lim moved so as to face him.

"Did the wine help?"

"A little. I must apologize for what happened. Blood was choking me and pain made me strike out."

"Errors to add to the rest."

Dumarest said, "You talk in riddles. I'm hurt and could be

dying. Have someone help me to my cabin and send for medical aid."

"You will not die." Lim was confident. "Not for a long
time. And you will have everything you need for your comfort if you will just do one small thing." He stepped forward
and placed a sheet of paper together with a stylo on the table.
"Just write down the correct sequence of the units forming
the affinity twin."

"What?" Dumarest looked blank. "What the hell are you
talking about?"

"Fifteen units," mused the cyber. "Millions of possible
combinations and it will take millennia to make and test
them all. But you have the secret and you will give it to me."

"You?"

"The Cyclan. It belongs to us. It was stolen from us. Now
write. Waste no more time."

Dumarest coughed a spatter of blood over the paper.
"You're mad," he said. "Mad!"

"Let us end this farce." Lim's voice did not change its even
modulation but the freshly washed face tautened a little, became more like a skull. "When she left for Zabul Carina
Davaranch carried no drugs. Obviously she must have obtained them after landing. But from where? And why should
she anticipate the need? My instructions were firm and covered all eventualities. By my orders Dumarest had been
stripped and wore nothing but a thin robe. Aside from physical violence the woman had nothing to fear and she was
armed against that." The laser lifted in his hand. "She could
have crippled the man, seared his eyes, done anything as long
as she did not hurt his brain or endanger his life. And the
forces of Zabul were with her. They had no reason to risk the
safety of their world for a stranger."

"So?"

"An ampule. A red ampule. Cattaneo saw it in your hand
when he entered the room. You claimed to have used it on
Dumarest. A possibility but there is another explanation."
Pausing, Lim added, "How did you get that puncture mark in
your neck?"

"An attack. I was struck."

"On the face but not on the throat. There is no sign of
bruising."

"You condemn me for that?"

"That and other things. The way you walk, for example; it is not easy to emulate a foreign stride. The way you attacked—no woman would use her fists in such a way. Your term of address—Carina Davaranch had more respect."

"I am she."

"Then tell me the number of your cabin."

A guess, he could only make a guess, but it was one he had to make. "Eleven."

"Eight. You see how you betray yourself?" The laser steadied to aim at Dumarest's right elbow. "You are not Carina Davaranch. There is only one other person you could be. Now, Earl Dumarest, write down the sequence of the affinity twin."

Dumarest said, "You're crazy. If I was the man you say, what the hell am I doing on the *Saito*?

The sac rested where it had been placed in the hold of the vessel, the figure beneath the transparent membrane lying as though dead. A strong, well-made body, the pale amber robe doing little to mask the contours of bone and muscle. The man for whom the Cyclan had hunted so long—or was it?

If Dumarest was in the woman's body then what was his own doing on the ship?

Lim turned, thoughtful, his face a mask as he assessed the probabilities. Dumarest was far from being stupid but this smacked of idiocy. Why use the affinity twin at all if he intended to board the *Saito*?

The answer could lie in his blindly instinctive attack which had so pathetically failed. To kill Lim and then to destroy the vessel and all within it. The same destruction freeing his intelligence from the host-body and allowing him to wake in his own. But, in that case, why bring his own body on the vessel? If he intended to destroy the ship how could he hope to avoid total erasure along with it?

"Master." Cattaneo bowed as he approached. "Is the sac to be opened and the man placed in the prepared cabin?"

The woman had been against it and her objections had made sense. But the woman was only a shell for the intelligence within, and Dumarest must have had his own reasons for not wanting the sac to be opened. Did it contain his body at all?

Logic dictated it did not. To have used the affinity twin to take over the woman's body and so gain access to the vessel made sense if his objective had been to destroy it. To transport his own body with him—no, there were too many objections against it. The figure within the sac had to be a dummy. But how had the exchange been accomplished?

To Cattaneo Lim said, "After you had placed Dumarest in the sac and sealed it what happened?"

"Nothing, master. We carried it from the room to the loading port." He added more details as Lim waited. "We walked ahead of the woman. I think she paused a moment to speak to someone, another woman, I think."

"Be certain." The man would never become a cyber. He entertained too many doubts.

"A woman," Cattaneo said after a moment's hesitation. "The burden was heavy," he explained. "And there were calls and abuse from some who were watching. Young people who were kept in line by guards."

"And?"

"That is all, master."

"You kept in personal physical contact with the sac at all times?"

"Yes. At least, almost."

"Explain." Lim condemned the man as he listened. To have neglected such an item in his initial report was beyond forgiveness. "An emergency during which you were blinded by dust, knocked into and separated from the sac—and you failed to mention it?"

"Master, it was a matter of seconds."

Long enough for an exchange to have been made and Lim was convinced that is what had happened. Dumarest here in the body of Carina Davaranch while his own rested safe in Zabul. To kill and destroy, then to return to the safety he had arranged.

A neat plan and one he could appreciate, pitiful as it was in its limitations. But how had Dumarest, locked in the physically weak body of a woman, hoped to destroy the ship and crew?

Hurt, unarmed, hampered by a foreign musculature—the failure of his attack proved how unfit he was. How then? How?

Lim looked at the sac, the figure it contained. A dummy, he was certain, but what else?

To Cattaneo he said, "Prepare for space. I want that sac to be removed to a point on the far side of Zabul and placed in a synchronic orbit. Use all the help you need but exercise the greatest care."

A bomb, Lim thought. It had to be a bomb. Explosives shaped and fashioned into the likeness of a man. Set with detonators and capable of blowing the *Saito* to dust. Already he could have left it too late.

The period of tension eased as the minutes passed and the sac was removed from the hold and the vicinity of the ship. Only when it was well clear did he return to the cabin where Dumarest was held.

It was a place of torment in which agony was king.

Dumarest looked at his hands, seared, crushed, broken, the fingers robbed for all time of their delicate skills. The wrists showed puckered wounds and both elbows ached from repeated blows. Acts performed with scientific detachment by a man with the smooth, uncaring face of an angel.

"Master." He turned as Lim entered the cabin, not bowing, but appearing to cringe. "As yet no success."

"Leave us." As the door closed behind him Lim said, "I would prefer to dispense with this barbarism but if necessary it can continue."

"Until I die?"

"Is that your objective?"

"Pain," said Dumarest. "Apply enough of it and you can make a saint plead to become a sinner. You are hardly subtle, cyber."

"And you are being wilfully stupid. What can continued refusal gain? You are here, alive, and will continue to be kept that way. In pain and torment, but alive. Where is your body?"

Dumarest shook his head. "I don't know what you're talking about."

"You insist on continuing the pretense but it is a waste of time. I know you used the affinity twin to take over the body of the woman. I know your body is somewhere in Zabul." Lim saw the sudden tension of the broken hands. "The dummy you brought here is now far distant in space. A bomb, of course. One which would be detonated when you stopped relaying a biological signal. Did you swallow a capsule to monitor the beating of your heart?" Again he saw the betraying movement of the hands. "You have been clever in a primitive fashion but now you see that cleverness was not enough. You are here. Your body is in Zabul. I shall demand it be handed over and will destroy the entire installation if it is not. Piece by piece, naturally, with due warning given as to which part is next. How many warnings will I have to give? How much destruction will they accept?"

Dumarest said, "Try it and they will blast you from space."

"So you admit your body is there?"

"I admit nothing. God! My hands!"

Twin furnaces of searing agony rose to fog his mind with a dull haze shot with brittle lightning. The pain diminished that in his chest by contrast. The man with the angelic face had known his trade.

"The sequence?"

"Go to hell!"

"No, Dumarest, it is you who will dwell in hell. The pain in your hands is nothing to what that body you are wearing can be made to suffer. A prelude to what will happen once your own body is in my hands. But, for now, the eyes, I think. Acid placed in each corner so as to burn out the orbs. Later we shall try the application of mental probes. Stimulation of the pain center of the brain will cause no physical damage but will yield unimaginable torment. The sequence?"

"My hands! I can't—"

"Write? Of course not. But you can gesture." Lim freed the broken appendages from their clamps. "Here." He placed a sheet on the table before Dumarest. It was marked with the fifteen molecular units. "Just point to each as they are to be united to form the chain."

Dumarest lifted a hand, blood dripping from the wounded fingers, touched the sheet and left only smears.

"Try again." Lim replaced the sheet with another, watching as, again, Dumarest failed.

"I can't. Give me something to point with. A stylo." Dumarest took it, fighting the pain as he forced torn flesh to obey, stabbed the point at the symbols one after the other. "There!"

"Do it again." Lim followed the pattern. It was the same but he had no way of telling if it was correct. "The acid, I think. It is important to be sure."

"No!" Dumarest sagged, a man trapped in an alien body, broken, pleading. "I want to help. You can check I'm telling the truth. On Zabul. I marked the sequence on my skin. In case I forgot. For God's sake don't hurt me again!"

"Your body?"

"In a casket. I'll show you!"

The obvious hiding place. Lim turned and touched the button of a communicator. "Captain? Take us at once to Zabul. Direct contact."

Moments yet before the ship could move. Time in which the cyber could check the situation—to realize the error he could have made. As Lim turned again to the communicator Dumarest lunged from the table.

He was slow, awkward, lacking strength and judgment but his objective was simple; to gain time. To prevent the cyber from canceling his order. Lim staggered as Dumarest slammed against him, falling back, hands lifting as Dumarest thrust the stylo at an eye. The blow missed, the point catching the skin at the side of the face, ripping it to mix blood with the ink. A struggle ended as the cyber struck back in turn to send Dumarest to the floor, there to lie in a raw tide of pain.

A red fury which dissolved in a gush of searing white flame.

Death was an ending, a release and, for him, a transition. Lying in the sac, Dumarest looked at the naked splendor of the galaxy beyond the taut membrane and wondered if it was always like that. But it had been Carina who had died—his turn was yet to come.

He reached for the controls and looked at the bulk of Zabul, at the dying haze beyond it where the *Saito* had been. A nimbus grew as the jets moved him toward the artificial world, fading in expanding vapor soon to be nothing but a host of spreading atoms. A pyre in which Lim had died, his acolytes, the crew and Carina Davaranch. Her genius deserved a better monument.

Suited figures moved toward the sac as it neared the port and within it Althea was waiting.

"Earl!" Her arms closed around him with unsuspected strength. "I thought you were dead. Earl!"

"Easy." The memory of lacerated lungs was too recent as

was that of broken hands. "You must have known I was safe. You saw the sac taken from the ship."

"Yes, but we didn't know you were in it. How—" She shook her head, baffled. "After all that trouble to get you why did they let you go?"

A gamble taken and won and he thought about it when, later, he sipped wine in the warm comfort of her room. At the last Lim must have known and it gave a special pleasure to remember his eyes, the shock of understanding. The recognition of his error must have given the cyber a foretaste of hell.

"A bomb," he explained as Althea sat at his side. "I made it and planted it against the hull. Kusche helped me to carry it and tampered with the fuses but I'd lied to him and he wasted his time. Even so it was proof of what I'd suspected."

"So you killed him?"

"No. Carina did that."

"The bitch! She almost laughed at me, Earl. When you were being carried to the port. I could have killed her!"

Instead she had done as he'd asked and never realized the conversation had been to remind her of what needed to be done.

Now, frowning, she said, "I still don't understand. Why the arranged accident? All we did was to sound the alarm and fill the air with dust and bump into those men carrying the sac."

A bluff and it had worked. Dumarest looked at his wine, thinking of the chance he had taken. The gamble which he'd been unable to avoid. His use of the affinity twin had been certain to be discovered but he had to make sure it was done in such a way as not to be obvious. And then, at the right moment, sow the doubt which had sent Lim on the one path which would rob the cyber of victory.

At the last, surely, he must have known.

Known there had been no time to make a dummy and switch it for the real man. Known that his own cautious logic had trapped him into falling a victim to the deception. Known too, at the last, that all Dumarest had done and said had been aimed at making him move the vessel once the sac was safely away.

The Erhaft field itself had detonated the bomb.

"Earl?" Althea touched his hand and smiled when he looked toward her. "I've been talking to some of the young ones. They aren't happy. They think as you do: the Council is too old and reluctant to change. Volodya tends to side with them."

"So?"

"To them you're a hero, Earl. More than that." Pausing she added, "They want you to guide them to Earth."